FEㅏ
CHILD

Che Golden has led a typical second-generation Irish life, spending most of her childhood shuttling backwards and forwards between London and Blarney, County Cork, trying to get people on both sides of the Irish Sea to pronounce her name properly. An ex-journalist, she has now settled permanently in Somerset with her husband and two children, blissfully making up whopping, complicated lies that sometimes turn into books.

THE
FERAL
CHILD

CHE GOLDEN

Quercus

First published in Great Britain in 2012 by Quercus

55 Baker Street
7th Floor, South Block
London
W1U 8EW

A CIP catalogue reference for this book is available
from the British Library

ISBN 978 1 85738 379 2

1 3 5 7 9 10 8 6 4 2

Printed and bound in Great Britain by Clays Ltd, St Ives plc.

For Paul,
who has a hard time believing in faeries
but always believed in me.

CHAPTER ONE

Maddy scowled and scuffed her trainers along the ground. Each time she saw a loose stone she aimed a vicious kick at it, pretending it was Danny's head that bounced along the street.

She was sick of living in Ireland, sick of Blarney and sick of her idiot cousins. She used to cry when she had to get back on the plane to return to London after visits to her grandparents. She snorted. What a baby she had been. Now London and all her friends might as well be on the other side of the world. She was stuck in tiny Blarney, in freezing County Cork, dealing with prats like Danny, one of the nastiest people you could meet this side of an Asbo.

What really annoyed her was that Danny was family, her cousin. But Danny and the rest of her cousins had been making it very clear for the last year they didn't have time for her. She gritted her teeth and felt her cheeks warm as she remembered Danny standing in front of her this afternoon, smirking at her. He was hitting his little sister Roisin and Maddy had made the mistake of standing up for her.

'This has got nothing to do with you, you blow-in,' he sneered. 'You're only here because your parents are dead and no one else wants you. Why don't you piss off back to England?'

'Trust me, mate, I would if I could,' she said, just before she punched him in the face. And what had Roisin said or done when Danny hit Maddy back and the fight started? Nothing! Wouldn't even look her in the eye.

Of course, all the adults thought the fight was her fault, seeing as she had thrown the first punch. No one seemed to care about provocation or extenuating circumstances. That's why she was wandering the road, walking a dog that normally walked itself, while her cousins got ready to go home. Granny had just handed her the dog's lead and pointed at the door. 'Don't you go into the castle now,' she had said, before she closed the door on Maddy. 'Walk him once around the square and then home.'

It amazed her, it really did, that her grandparents or her hideous aunts still thought she gave a toss about their rules or anything they had to say. It was *boring* walking George, her grandfather's black and white terrier. He didn't seem too impressed either. He hopped and bumped along behind her as she dragged him by his lead.

She stopped to look up at the ruined castle as it loomed over the tiny village of Blarney where her grandparents lived. George crashed into the back of her leg and huffed. She ignored him as she gazed up at the keep, its broken battlements letting long golden shafts of autumn sun break through. It looked like something from a faerie tale. Her grandfather was always trying to terrify her with tales of ghouls, ghosts and wicked faeries that lived in the grounds, who stole children and took them back to Faerie Land, never to be seen again. She snorted. As if.

'What do you say, boy?' she said to the dog. 'You don't want to go on a boring walk, do you? I bet *you* want to do something much more exciting.'

George barked and wagged his tail.

It was far too easy to crawl through a hole in the fence that separated the castle grounds from the car park, an overgrown bush hiding her from interfering grown-ups as she pulled George in after her.

She could see her grandfather talking to one of the groundsmen, Seamus Hegarty. Granda was the gatekeeper to the grounds but he didn't have much to do at this time of the evening – no one bought entry tickets this late. The path to the castle was lined with huge oak trees, and Maddy and George darted from one to another to keep well out of her grandfather's sight as he idled by the ticket booth. Then it curved into a bridge that crossed a sluggish river, evil-eyed pike cruising in its depths. Once Maddy and George had scooted over the bridge they were safe, and they ran toward the broken-toothed tower of the castle, in the opposite direction to the tourists who chattered and stopped only to take last-minute photos.

Its grey walls leached any warmth from the weak autumn sun, and its shadow lay heavy and clammy. Water seeped constantly down its rough-hewn stones, and ferns flourished at its base. Ivy clung to the lower reaches, leaves lapping at the rock's sweat. The castle squatted and squinted with arrow-slit eyes at the fields and woods before it. A cave nestled deep into its roots yawned as Maddy jogged past, the damp air that fanned from it as cold as corpse breath.

But it wasn't the castle Maddy was interested in, with its retinue of ghosts. Instead, she headed for a little tunnel dug into the hill at the foot of the castle that led to some very strange landscaped gardens. Grown-ups had to bend almost double to walk through, but Maddy jogged along comfortably, the top of her head just brushing the wet stone.

Years ago, someone had decided to give the tourists a taste of old Ireland with a faerie kingdom. The tunnel opened up into a world of moss-covered evergreens and cool ferns that nodded next to the gurgling river. It had wooden signposts with Celtic-style lettering that pointed out things like 'The Witch's Cave', 'The Wishing Steps' and 'The Faerie Mound'. It was guarded by crows who screamed in the branches and glared down at Maddy with their cruel black eyes.

Her cousins thought the place was naff and that she was a baby for liking it so much. *They must think I'm thick*, thought Maddy, *if they think I don't know the faerie mound is a just a pile of earth created by a JCB.* Just like she knew the witch's cave had been built by the bricklayer who lived next door to her grandparents.

She let George off the lead and left the path for the gloom of the woods. George ran after her with his tail wagging. The birds were roosting in the trees and she could hear the faint sound of a bell ringing in the grounds, a warning that the gates would soon be locked. But she ignored it – she still had a few minutes before it was completely dark, and she could always let herself back out through the hole in the fence.

She sat with her back to a gnarled pine tree and brooded. It wasn't a good thing to do; she knew that. Her teacher was always telling her to rise above things, to think good thoughts when she was having a bad day, but clearly the woman didn't have a clue if she thought that worked. The hurt and the anger soured in Maddy's stomach. Everything Danny had said today, everything her cousins said any day, kaleidoscoped through her mind. Every time she tried to join in with a game or a discussion it was always the same. They shrugged her off with 'Who cares what you think?' or 'Who cares what you want?'

She missed London. She missed the lights and the traffic and the people. London was alive, it had energy that fizzed up through the concrete to the soles of her feet. Blarney didn't even have a Pizza Hut. She couldn't tell anyone that though. They'd think she was being a stuck-up Londoner, trying to act like she was better than them.

'Well, I am,' she said aloud in the gathering gloom. 'London is better than this dump any day of the week.' She stood up and yelled at the top of her lungs, 'I'M FROM THE INDEPENDENT REPUBLIC OF LONDON!' Her shouts sent crows flurrying into the sky, cawing with annoyance. She laughed, her voice flat with the dull edge of her anger.

George looked at her with what she thought was an accusatory stare in his narrow brown eyes.

'I know I look like a psycho,' she said, 'but everyone

keeps telling me I'll feel better if I let it all out, so if you don't like it, ask Santa to bring me a punchbag.'

The dog's face and sides twitched like he was trying to spit a reply out and then he twisted around and started to chase a flea through his fur with yellowed fangs.

She sighed. The sun was sinking. It was just a sliver of red on the horizon, a sore spot in a turquoise sky. Beneath the trees it was already night.

She was about to walk home when a rabbit came hopping out of the undergrowth. It froze when it spotted George, who got to his feet and stretched his neck in anticipation. Too late, the rabbit tried to make a run for it, and before she could grab him George tore after the animal, his little legs blurring as he gave chase.

'George, NO!'

He was gone before she had run more than a few steps.

'Oh, marvellous,' yelled Maddy. 'Just bloody marvellous!'

She was really for it now – her grandparents were going to kill her for losing that dozy dog. She sighed. It was getting too dark to search for him. She was better off going back to her grandparents' house and hoping the terrier would come home when he was hungry. A bad end to a really bad day.

'Why are you so angry?' said a voice close to her ear.

She jumped out of her skin with fright and looked around to see a little red-haired boy standing beside her. She hadn't heard him creep up on her, and she glared at him.

'Where the bloody hell did you come from?' she asked.

The boy widened glass-green eyes at her and twisted his lips. 'Do your mummy and daddy know you swear like that? Mine would never allow me.'

She stared at him for a second while her heart twisted in her chest. Was it possible that there was someone in this village who did not know why Maddy's parents couldn't care less about her language? Her throat hardened with tears. She couldn't trust herself to speak so she clambered to her feet and walked away. But the boy trotted to catch her up and angled his head to gaze up into Maddy's lowered face.

'Why are you crying?'

'It's none of your business.'

'You are very rude. I'm only trying to be nice to you.'

'Well, I'm not in the mood, so bog off and leave me alone,' snapped Maddy.

She carried on walking and calling for the dog, straining her ears for any sound of George. She dug her nails into her palms and prayed the dog would come back in the next five minutes. But there was no sign of him, and her new pal wasn't taking the hint either. She could hear boy's feet scuffing the dead leaves as he walked after her, and she sighed loudly when he started talking again.

'My name is John, by the way. You can come and play with me, if you like. I've got a toy gun and a bow and arrow – we could take turns playing cowboys and Indians.'

'No, thanks,' said Maddy.

'We don't have far to go. I live in here.'

'Don't tell lies, you freak. No one lives in here.'

'I'm not, and I do. Where are your parents?'

'None of your bus—'

'Do your parents live with you? Are they waiting for you at home?' he interrupted.

She gritted her teeth and zipped her jacket against the autumn chill. *Bog off, bog off, bog off, you PRAT!* she snarled inside her head.

Perhaps she should have said it out loud because now he was rummaging through his pockets and pulling out a white paper bag. 'Would you like a sweet?'

'Are you special needs or something?' said Maddy. 'I mean, do I look like I'm friendly? Do I look like I'm in the market for a new pal?'

The boy cocked his head on one side. 'You feel very lonely.'

That was it. *Feel* was a trigger word for Maddy. Anger bubbled up like molten lava in her throat and she swung around and pushed her face into his, her hands balled into fists. 'You know how I *feel*, do you? What a relief – I really need someone to tell me how I'm feeling. Here, pal, how does this *feel*?' She hammered her fists against his chest, a half-punch, half-shove that normally sent most kids staggering backwards, while the anger popped and fizzed in her mouth.

But John didn't even grunt as her hands thumped out a dull note on his ribcage. He only grinned at her, flashing very sharp white teeth. 'How delicious – anger too.'

Something wasn't right here, and if she hadn't been so busy being angry she might have noticed it sooner. Like the fact that no one normal played cowboys and Indians at her age or called their parents 'Mummy' and 'Daddy'. She watched him licking his lips, his unblinking eyes locked on hers. 'That's it, you nut job, I'm out of here,' she said.

As she turned to go, she felt his hand clamp on to her arm. His nails were digging through her jacket and she was shocked at how strong he was for such a skinny kid. The white paper bag fell from his grasp, and as the sweets tumbled on to the grass, she thought she saw the green blades turn black.

'There's something else as well,' he said, sniffing the air like a dog. 'Something older and riper under all that anger. Ah, yes.' He fixed his eyes on hers again. 'Despair. A deep, deep pit of despair.'

She tried to jerk her arm away but he didn't even flinch. 'Let go of me,' she hissed.

'Why would I do that, when you are such a rare find?' He smiled and tipped his head to one side again as he looked at her. 'Such rage and hatred in a child. Life just isn't worth living, is it?'

Maddy went cold. Kids didn't talk like that. *No one* talked like that. She tried to pull away, but he had a tight hold on both her upper arms now and began drawing her back toward the shadows. Her mouth went dry with fear and she twisted around, pulling out of one of his hands, and tried to swing a punch, but he dropped her other arm and caught her fist in the palm of his hand. Then he began to crush her fingers and bear down on her upraised arm with all his weight. She screamed as the pain rocketed toward her elbow and her knees buckled underneath her. He bent down until his face was close to hers. His glass-green eyes seemed to float toward her, hanging in front of her sweat-streaked face like glowing balls.

'If you stop struggling, it will be much easier,' he said. He wasn't even out of breath.

Maddy froze. 'What will be easier?'

'Coming with me, of course.'

She looked up at him and fear turned her stomach to ice as she realized what he meant. *It's happening*, she thought. *It's actually happening. I'm being abducted and it's not some creepy old man doing it; it's a really creepy kid.*

She began to cry as he forced her down on to the earth until her free hand was splayed among the leaves as she fought to stay upright, her other arm burning in its socket. Her tears mingled with her sweat and filled her mouth with salt. She thought of the street lights, the noisy pub, the people out walking their dogs, and her grandparents sitting in their living room, wondering where she was. The whole of bright, breathing Blarney village was only a hundred metres away on the other side of the castle fence. She wished she hadn't come in here, wished she was sitting down to dinner with her grandparents right now, with George eating noisily from his bowl in the corner. She could not stop looking into the strange boy's eyes. Her body went numb. She could hear the crows screaming, but when she opened her own mouth only a hoarse croak escaped.

What was wrong with her? The trees loomed over her, pressing close. The world swayed and shuddered at the edge of her darkening vision. She thought she heard laughter floating on the air and bells tinkling as the undergrowth shivered. Her head tipped back on her shoulders, only John's glass-green eyes glowing bright and clear as the rest of the world blurred. 'I want to go home,' she slurred as her thick tongue rolled in her mouth. 'I want to go home.'

John shook his head. 'I don't think so. You're going to play with me for a while. I can spin you a necklace of spider webs. We can hide in the trees and watch the wild hunt pass by.'

She moaned in terror. He bared his teeth at her in a mockery of a smile. 'We are going to have such fun.'

A little blur of black and white streaked out of the dark, leaped and sank its teeth into John's hand. There was a split second of stunned silence as George twisted in the air, stubby legs paddling, before the boy shook him off on to the ground. John backed away from the little terrier, who stood in front of Maddy with his legs planted wide apart, yellow teeth bared and the hair on his back standing on end.

The boy looked down at his mauled hand, at the blood running down his arm and dripping on to the leafy ground. His eyes narrowed into slits, and his breathing was harsh and loud through his open mouth. Maddy didn't think he looked like a little boy any more. He looked horribly, horribly old. She hugged her aching arm to her side and sobbed with relief that the pain was gone.

She began to scramble back and climb to her feet when he raised his hands and started to shriek. The undergrowth erupted around them as hidden things rushed toward her. Maddy didn't wait to see what was coming. She ran.

She could hear John screaming behind her, and he was getting closer. There was an angry hum in the air, and as her feet found the broad smooth path that led to the entrance gate and the car park Maddy could hear a sound like fat raindrops falling on leaves. It sounded like feet.

She ran faster, her breath burning her lungs, her heart squeezed tight with fear. 'Don't look behind, don't look behind, don't look behind,' she chanted. She offered up the silent prayer of desperate children everywhere: *PleaseGodpleaseGodpleaseGodgetmeoutofthis-andIwillbegoodpromisepromisepromise.*

George found the gap in the fence. She saw the white tip of his tail disappear and threw herself after it.

As she wriggled through, a hand clutched the heel of her trainer and began to tug. She screamed and clawed at the ground, breaking her nails on the concrete, trying to drag her way out as the hand grabbed her ankle. She kicked back hard and felt a crunch, heard a squeal. She squirmed out of the gap and into the car park. She was up and sprinting again as soon as she hit tarmac, but had not gone more than a few strides when she ran into something a lot bigger and wider than she was. An inky blackness closed around her face and stopped her breath; she screamed again and beat at it with her fists, only to be swung high into the air to find herself staring down at her grandfather.

CHAPTER TWO

'Here you are! And why do I find you here? How many times have you been told not to go into the castle,' he shouted, his face puce with anger . 'You could break your neck in there in the dark!'

Maddy was too shocked to do anything but stare at him as her breath came in frightened gulps. George was barking at the hole in the fence, the hair on his back still standing on end.

Granda put her down. 'What is going on with the pair of you?'

'There was a boy in there,' said Maddy. 'He was really weird and he tried to pull me into the trees. George bit him and we ran for it, and I think there were other people chasing us as well.'

Granda whistled for George, but the little terrier didn't seem to hear him. 'Come here, George, you eejit!' he shouted, and the dog reluctantly slunk to his side.

'A boy, you say?'

Maddy nodded.

'What did he look like?'

'He had red hair, green eyes, about my height. He said he lived in the castle. But no one lives in the castle grounds, do they?'

'What did he say his name was?'

'John. Do you know him, Granda? Does he live in there?'

Granda stared at the fence and rubbed his stubble with the palm of his hand. The red drained from his face, leaving him jaundiced under the sulphur glow of the street light. 'Let's go find your granny; she has been worried out of her mind over you.' He turned on his heel and strode off toward the village square, clearly expecting Maddy and George to trot after him in the wake of his long, billowing coat. Maddy stood there with her mouth agape. Someone had just tried to kidnap her, and Granda wanted to go home for dinner?

'Where are you going?' she yelled at his back. 'Why aren't you going to find that boy and that weird cult he's probably hanging out with? We need to do something!'

'Time enough for that in the morning. I'm sure he's long gone by now.'

'Are you at least going to call the police?'

'No point,' said the old man. He turned to look at her.

'Don't you think you're overreacting, Maddy? You got into a fight with another child, and now he's a member of a cult? This is Blarney. I think we would notice if something like that was going on.'

'So you know who that boy is then?'

'I know *of* him,' he said. 'There's no need to involve the police.'

She glared at the old man. 'You don't believe me. You think I'm lying.'

'Maddy, don't be starting another fight. I really could do without it tonight.'

'Fine, be like that!' Maddy started running, ignoring Granda's shouts. George chased after her as she tore down the lane toward the row of terraced cottages that framed one side of the village square. The little one-storey houses were lit up, their warm yellow lights puddling on the tarmac of the road. The chip shop on the side that faced the castle was ablaze with light and packed with teenagers. The night lights of the supermarket next to it cast sharp shadows on the grass of the square, while the side that faced her grandparents had the comforting presence of the Garda Siochana station, with its blue light above the door, and Blarney Hotel, where the bar was doing a good trade tonight. They all looked so inviting, standing against the dark and silent castle, and Maddy's legs went weak with relief as she realized she was safe.

Until she saw her grandmother standing in the doorway with her hands on her hips. She looked really, really angry. Maddy slowed to a walk. If she could, she would have reversed.

'It doesn't take much to guess where you have been all this time while your supper has been getting cold,' she said as Maddy and George tried to squeeze past her. 'You have been told a million times if you have been told once, young lady, that you are not to go into the castle on your own. And that fool of a dog not even on a lead – what would happen if a car came?'

Maddy knew it was not a good idea to be a smart-mouth, but by now it was a reflex action. 'Duh – he'd be killed.'

Her grandmother was not amused. She drew herself up to her full height – all five feet and one inch – and pointed into the house. 'In. That dog is to go out to his kennel right now and you're to get yourself washed before dinner. And look at the state of your jeans, covered in muck. You have me ashamed of my life, going around the road like that . . .'

Her grandmother's scolding voice drifted after Maddy as she walked through the house. She let George out into the garden. There was a metal chain attached to his kennel and she clipped the free end to his collar. Granda's two big hunting hounds, Pedlar and Bewley, poked their noses out of their kennels and huffed sleepily. George whined and licked Maddy's nose.

'Sorry, boy,' she whispered. 'We're both in the dog-house tonight.'

'Maddy,' piped a high voice. 'Maddy, Maddy, Mad-deeeee.'

She looked over her shoulder at the garden wall and smiled. Straining to see over it was a two-year-old boy with a plastic dinosaur gripped in one fist.

'Hi, Stephen,' she said.

'Maddy, Maddy, what do-a?' he asked.

'Not much,' she said.

'Come play!'

Maddy really wanted to chill out with a DVD, but the cynic in her looked at Stephen's golden-blond hair and big blue eyes – he would make an excellent buffer between her and Granny.

'Ask your mum first, and then we can play in my house,' she said.

'Mammy says "yes",' called a woman's voice. Mrs Forest, Stephen's mother, was smiling indulgently at her son from the kitchen doorway. 'Just for an hour, and then he needs to get to bed.'

Maddy grinned as Stephen jumped up and down, shrieking with excitement. She leaned over the wall and scooped him up by the armpits, kissing the top of his head as he wrapped his legs around her waist. He was soft and cuddly in his pyjamas and dressing gown, his chubby feet swallowed up by Mickey Mouse slippers. She nuzzled his hair and breathed deep. He had just had a bath and smelt of shampoo and baby oil. As she walked up the garden with him balanced on her hip he chattered nonsense to her, waving the dinosaur around for emphasis. She had to whip her head out of range a couple of times to avoid getting hit in the face.

'We have a visitor,' she said as she walked into the kitchen.

Granny turned from the oven and smiled at Stephen before narrowing her eyes at Maddy.

'I bet you think you're awful cute, don't you?' she asked.

Maddy widened her eyes in mock innocence. 'Who, me?'

Granny shot her one of her looks before smiling down at Stephen again.

'Are you hungry, peteen?'

'Oh for God's sake, don't be stuffing him. He's probably just had dinner,' said Maddy, but Stephen nodded his head.

'Would you like a sugar sandwich?'

'Oh yuck!' Maddy pulled a face while Stephen crowed with delight. 'He's going to grow up deformed if you keep giving him rubbish like that to eat.'

'It never did you any harm,' snapped Granny.

'That we know of,' muttered Maddy, stomping into the living room.

She refused to speak to either of her grandparents while she ate her dinner – Stephen filled the awkward silence with his chatter. Her grandparents only had the one reception room, which was dominated by a square dining table. They had an armchair each, either side of a big black range where a fire burned merrily, and the sofa was pushed under the window, behind one of the armchairs. No one ever used it – it was just a dumping ground for coats and newspapers. There wasn't much space for Maddy to sit in here if she wasn't at the table so she usually kept to her room. There was no hallway in the cottage – the front door opened straight into the living room – so she was never far away from the action, but Granny would not let her eat in the bedroom. *Fine by me*, she thought. *I can handle bad vibes much better than these two. No one cares that I get bullied and was nearly kidnapped. There should be a policeman here right now.*

Granda was the first to crack. He had settled himself into his chair with a newspaper and when Granny banged Maddy's plate down in front of her, he looked over the top of the paper and pulled a face at them both to make them laugh. Stephen giggled, but Maddy gave Granda a filthy look from the corner of her eye.

'You're nowhere near as big as you like to think you are, Maddy, but carry on like this and I'll soon put a stop to your gallop,' said Granny as she settled into a dining chair opposite. Maddy looked at Granny's left ear and deliberately unfocused her eyes. That always drove Granny crazy.

'Look at me when I'm talking to you, or there will be no TV all weekend,' said Granny.

'No Shrek!' wailed Stephen, his eyes brimming with tears.

'Not you, pet,' soothed Granny, and the little boy smiled and carried on eating his sandwich.

Yeah, right. It was all talk. Maddy had been living here a year and neither of her grandparents had ever disciplined her.

'I would have been home a lot sooner if that boy hadn't stopped me,' she said.

'What boy?' asked Granny.

'It's nothing, Maureen. Children's foolishness,' said Granda. 'Best not to get involved. Otherwise it will turn into World War Three.'

Maddy could have flung her plate at him. Foolishness?! Her right hand was stiff and turning purple with bruises.

It hurt, actually hurt, to hold her knife to cut her food. She was sure a nice set of bruises was developing on her arms as well, not to mention the fact that the boy had scared the living daylights out of her.

'What boy?' Granny asked again, glaring at Maddy.

'I got into a fight with some kid who claims he lives in the castle grounds and then tried to *kidnap me*, but *apparently* it's no big deal,' said Maddy, sarcasm dripping from her tongue.

Granny narrowed her eyes at her. 'What do you mean, he tried to kidnap you?'

'He was trying to pull me into the trees. Said it would be easier if I went with him.'

'Did he ask you to play?' asked Granda.

Maddy looked at him out of the corner of her eye. 'Yeah.'

'And you said no, I suppose?'

'What's that got to do with anything?' said Maddy.

Granda sighed. 'It means he was upset you didn't want to play, not that he was trying to kidnap you. Why would a child kidnap another child? It doesn't make sense.'

Maddy looked down at her plate and scowled. Her arm ached way too much for that boy to be considered merely *upset*.

Granny tutted. 'All the same, a boy bullying a little

girl – I am sure his mother is very proud of what she's rearing,' she said. 'Bartholomew Kiely, first thing in the morning you're going to find out who that boy is, and I am going round to have a word with his mother.' Granda grunted and rattled the paper.

Maddy smirked. *Justice.*

Stephen had been staring at them while they argued, his big blue eyes wide. Maddy stroked his hair while she ate with one hand and he licked his plate for any loose sugar. Now he was making his dinosaur march along the pattern, roaring loudly, while Maddy made as much noise as she could scraping up the last of her dinner.

She could see Granny's lips thinning in irritation, but Granda tried to make peace. 'Come here to me, peteen, and I'll tell you a story,' he said, putting down his paper and holding an arm out to her.

Maddy shook her head and glared up at him from beneath her unruly mop of brown hair. 'Not in the mood.'

Granny tutted. 'A wee story won't hurt.'

'Godzilla, Godzilla!' squealed Stephen, banging his plastic dinosaur on the tabletop.

Maddy looked at Stephen and sighed. There would be no putting him off now – he would cry if he didn't get a story. She pushed her chair back from the table and patted her lap. 'Come and park your bum,' she said.

Stephen toddled over and climbed up on to her lap. He crossed his legs and leaned his head against her chest, popping a thumb into his mouth. She put her arms around him and wrapped her fingers around his bare ankles. They were cold, but Stephen didn't seem to have noticed.

'Did I ever tell you the story of Jenny Green Teeth who lives in the river that runs through the village?' asked Granda.

Maddy rolled her eyes. 'Yes,' she sighed, but it didn't stop him. Maddy spent the next half an hour listening to stories of elves and sprites and all manner of things that go bump in the night, all of whom seemed to live in the castle grounds. It was so obvious, it was tragic. *Does he not get that it doesn't stop me going in there?* she thought. The castle was cool and free of the village idiots that lived around here and populated her family. Her fingertips traced circles on Stephen's baby-soft skin, wondering at the feel of his tiny ankle bones.

She was beginning to doze off in the heat of the fire, Stephen's head lolling against her chest, when Granda gave her a nudge.

'Are you listening to me, Maddy?'

'Yes.'

'Then tell me the rules.'

'What rules?' asked Maddy as she knuckled at her eyes.

'What do you do if you meet a faerie?'

'This is stupid. I want to go to bed.'

'After you tell me the rules,' said Granda.

Maddy sighed and thought for a second. 'Never run, because they like to chase.'

'Good girl,' said Granda. 'What's next?'

'Don't eat or drink with them.'

'Because . . .' he prompted.

'Because you will never be satisfied with mortal food again. Don't listen to their music or dance with them either, because their idea of getting down with the homies is apparently so awesome that you'll stare at them like you're brain-damaged for months on end.'

'Be serious,' he said.

She looked at him. 'We're talking about *faeries*.'

'And they are always listening, so be respectful,' warned Granda. 'What else?'

She sighed again and looked into the fire, Stephen's sleepy weight was warm and comfortable in her arms. She wished Granda wouldn't try so hard to make her believe this stuff. She rattled off the rest of the rules in a bored monotone. 'Never make a vow with them, and never strike a bargain, because they don't make deals unless it's in their favour, and always wear iron, because it hurts them.'

'Good girl.' Granda gave her a kiss on the cheek.

'Bedtime for this little one, I think,' said Granny. She leaned down and prised a sleeping Stephen out of Maddy's arms, his dinosaur still clutched tight in one dimpled hand. His heavy lids blinked open once and his head fell against Granny's shoulder as he snored softly. 'I'll bring him home while you get ready for bed. Mary will be missing him.'

Later that evening, as Maddy was lying in bed half asleep, her bedroom door swung open. Granda was a dark shape in the doorway, blocking the soft glow of the lamps in the sitting room.

'A little something to help you sleep,' he whispered.

'George!' she squealed, as the terrier bounced into the room and jumped on to the bed. He cuddled into the crook of her arm. Maddy was delighted to have him in with her, but Granda never, ever allowed a dog in the house, and he really must have had to argue with Granny to let her have George in her bed. She could hear pots and pans being banged about in the kitchen, which meant Granny was not happy. Something was going on.

'You do believe me, about what happened with that boy, don't you?' she asked.

'I do, pet, but there is no point worrying your

grandmother,' he said. 'I've got something for you. It used to be mine when I was your age.' He pulled a necklace from his pocket and bent down to tie the clasp around her neck. It was a little iron cross, cold and rough on her skin. Maddy fingered it, a frown puckering between her eyes.

'You don't really believe in all that stuff about faeries, do you?' she asked.

Granda smiled. 'I think you should believe in everything, and then nothing can surprise you.'

'Really? So you've got the whole Allah-, Buddha-, Vishnu-thing going on as well then? Interesting. I must tell Father Damian the next time we're at Mass.'

He laughed. 'Don't be cheeky.' His face turned serious again. 'You know the Samhain Fesh is only two days away?'

'You mean Halloween?'

'I mean Samhain – some of us still remember the old ways, and if you want to make a claim on being Irish, you should get to know your history.'

'I've never made a claim on being Irish – I'm a Londoner,' said Maddy stiffly.

'London is where you lived; this is where you are from,' said Granda.

Maddy shrugged. She wasn't getting into this argument again. 'What about it?'

'According to the old tales, the boundaries between the faerie realm, Tír na nÓg, and the human world break down around now. It means faeries are stronger and they can walk among us. So, just for a little while . . .'

'I know, don't go into the castle. I don't know why you can't just say that, instead of making up all this faerie stuff. I'm not a baby.'

'I *do* tell you, Maddy, all the time, but you don't pay attention.'

'I don't get scared by the faerie stories either, but it doesn't stop you telling them.'

Granda sighed and pinched the bridge of his nose. He only did that when he was trying really hard to be patient and not yell. 'Just this once, Maddy, listen to me and keep yourself safe. Anything could happen in those grounds, and no one would know where you were.'

'OK,' she said in a small voice.

Her grandfather went to leave the room but turned with his hand on the doorknob.

'There is one other rule, Maddy – well, more of a warning really.'

'What's that?'

'Whatever a faerie promises you, whatever they try to tempt you with, it's not real. You have to trust your heart, not your eyes, and turn your feet for home.'

'Cheers. I'll remember that as I try to sleep in the dark.'

'Goodnight, love. Sleep well.'

'I'm going to have nightmares after all that,' Maddy muttered to George as the bedroom door clicked shut behind Granda, but the terrier was already snoring.

Great, she thought. *I don't have earplugs.*

CHAPTER THREE

Maddy was having trouble sleeping. Her arm was hurting and she was still upset that Granda didn't seem to be interested in punishing the boy who had done this to her. He always stuck up for her, so she didn't understand why he wasn't marching around to John's house and banging on the door. *Maybe he's finally getting sick of me*, she thought. She didn't want to live here, but if her grandparents didn't want her any more, it meant living with one of her mother's sisters. Maddy fancied that even less.

She lay on her back and listened to the sound of the village. There was no pavement outside her grandparents' house, and passing cars hummed by right outside her window. The beams of their headlights pierced the thin cotton of her bedroom curtains and swept across the walls. Now and then she could hear talking and laughter and the click of a woman's heels as people walked back from the pub. One couple stopped for a snog and Maddy gagged at the wet sound. *Why would anyone let someone stick their tongue in their mouth?* she thought. *Gross!* George had his nose tucked in her armpit and the amount of noise coming out of such a small dog was unbelievable. His nose whistled at the end of each snore and he was farting – a lot. Maddy was keeping the sheet stretched tight across her face to give her some breathable air. Having him in bed with her wasn't such a treat after all.

She heard the creak of her grandparents' bed through the wall behind her head as they settled down for the night. The pub closed, the chip shop shut its doors and turned off the lights and the night grew dark and silent. But Maddy could still only doze fitfully. The glow of the street light outside threw the shadows of the trees that lined the square over her bed and walls. She watched shadow branches reach for her with knotted arthritic fingers, skinny versions of Granny's tortured hands. The wind grew stronger and tossed the branches into strange shapes, but one kept appearing over and over again: a witch's face, with a hooked nose and chin and a toothless mouth. Maddy stared at it with wide eyes that were scratchy from lack of sleep. She kept telling herself it was just a tree, but the way that toothless mouth muttered and gabbled at her as the wind rose to a moan made her feel like a toddler who was frightened of the dark.

But she must have slept eventually because she was startled awake by George's rumbling growl and a weird noise at the window. Something was scraping the glass, long strokes down the length of the pane that hissed in the quiet of her room. She put a hand on George to get him to be quiet, but the dog still kept his black lips peeled back from his teeth as Maddy crawled across the bed to the windowsill. Her curtains were hung on a pole, leaving a slight gap between the fabric and the window, enough for her to peer out without touching the cloth, if she pressed her face hard against the wall.

She could feel the cold puff of a draught on her lips and see a sliver of the outside world with her left eye, the pearly glow of the white-painted sill and a slice of the velvety dark beyond it. But it was enough. There was someone at her window all right, someone with a long white hand that seemed to have too many joints and yellow pointed fingernails. The hand rose and trailed the tips of the fingernails down the glass, over and over again. Maddy's eye rose and fell with the hand as she huddled against the wall, her skin in goosebumps from the cold. Then it stopped. The hand fell out of sight and there was silence. Maddy held her breath, her heart thudding in her ears as she listened for any noise that would tell her who was outside.

Suddenly a bright green eye appeared right in front of her and stared into her own.

Maddy screamed and scrambled back from the window as George rushed toward it, barking. She grabbed him and clamped a hand over his muzzle. But George was ready for a fight and his hair bristled against her arm while his whole body jerked with imploding barks. Maddy's heart hammered in her chest and she caught her breath in shallow gulps. She could hear her grandparents muttering and the bed creaking as they turned over in their sleep. Then, there it was, a horrible sound.

Tap, tap, tap.

Whoever was outside her window, they knew she was listening.

Tap, tap, tap, went the fingernails against the glass.

Maddy listened to the persistent tapping and thought about that green eye. She grinned. She had a good idea who it belonged to. It was that boy from the castle. What was he doing, creeping about in the dark, trying to scare her at this time of night? But she was going to show him. If he thought she was a girly girl who was going to cry, he had another thing coming. She let George go. He lay flat against the bed and vibrated with growls as she eased her legs over the side and stepped across to the window. She clenched the curtains in her fists and wrenched them open.

She jumped back as if she had been burnt, colliding with the chest of drawers next to her bed. A corner scraped her thigh and she clamped her hand over her mouth to stop herself crying out in pain and fear.

It was John all right. But he looked very, very different. There was the red hair, the cute freckles and the green eyes. But the face was pointed into a little muzzle and his upturned nose looked like a pig's snout. The eyes were cruel and slanted, and the hands looked veiny and old. His ears were long, pointed and tipped with soft, fine hair. They swivelled toward her like a bat's as his nose snuffled at the window. He pressed a knobbly hand flat against the glass and smiled at her with long hooked teeth that seemed too big for the rosebud mouth.

'Come out and play with me,' he said. 'I'm so lonely in the dark.'

This is not happening, thought Maddy, as her heart gave up running and jumped into her throat to hide. *This is just not happening! Granda was right!*

Tap, tap, tap again with the cruel nails that looked more like claws. 'Let me in,' he whispered. 'Open the window and we can play.'

She shook her head and whimpered into her fingers. The smile on the faerie's face faded and then he spotted the iron cross hanging over her nightdress. He hissed, his face twisting with anger.

'So you See me now, little girl,' he said, pressing his face against the glass and fogging it with his breath. 'Who gave you the iron? Who do you know who has the Sight? Tell me now and I'll be merciful and only blind you.'

'Go away,' squeaked Maddy, her teeth chattering with fear. 'Go away.'

He snarled at her through the glass and then his eyes flicked to the left. He looked back at her, smiled an evil smile and suddenly dropped out of sight.

She stared at the blank window, waiting for him to pop up again like a demented jack-in-the-box. She didn't want to get too close to the glass. George cocked his head to one side, listening, his entire body stiff. She couldn't hear anything and nothing moved outside, but she didn't believe he would give up so easily. And what had he spotted? What did he know that she didn't? *Did he find a way in?* She shivered, her pyjamas sticking to the cold sweat on her back.

George began to growl again and then she heard it, a soft crooning noise, like someone singing a lullaby. Her skin crawled as she touched the window's cold surface, but she forced herself to press her face against it so she could see what he was up to.

There he was, just a metre to the left, outside the neighbours' house, crooning a wordless song and swaying in the moonlight. She heard a child's giggle, and her blood ran cold as it dawned on her *whose* window the creature was singing at.

Stephen. Stephen Forest is listening to him.

'No,' she whispered. 'Please, no.' She heard the unmistakable sound of a sash window being opened and saw the faerie smile and hold out his hand, still singing. A little white arm, still with traces of baby fat, reached out and grasped the fingers.

'NO!' Maddy began to scream and pound the window with her fists. 'No, leave him alone. LEAVE HIM ALONE!'

CHAPTER FOUR

Maddy ran into her grandparents' room and yelled loud enough to wake the dead.

'Get up, get up, you have to help him!'

Her grandparents looked completely bewildered and a little scared, blinking their eyes against the sudden light. Maddy flicked the switch on and off really fast to make sure they got the message.

'For goodness sake, child, whatever is the matter?' said Granny as she fumbled for her glasses.

'That boy, the one who beat me up, he followed me home, he's taken Stephen. GET UP!'

Her grandparents tumbled out of bed and staggered after her, pulling on their dressing gowns as they came into her room, where George was going ballistic. His legs were tense with rage and his volley of barks was lifting him off his feet. Maddy ran to the window and pointed to the disappearing figure of the twisted boy as he hurried toward the castle grounds. He was hunched over, and Maddy thought she could see the gleam of Stephen's blond hair in his arms as they passed beneath a street light.

'There, see, it's that boy, only he's not a boy,' she said. 'He wanted me to let him in but I wouldn't and then he went to Stephen's window and Stephen listened to him and now he's taken him. Look, look, over there, he's heading for the castle!'

Granny peered out of the window. 'I can't see who that is, Maddy, but I tell you now, I can't see Stephen. George, WILL YOU SHUT UP! And what do you mean, he isn't a boy?'

'He was really weird-looking. His face had gone all funny and he had these long pointed ears like you see on pixies.' She looked at Granda. 'He saw the cross around my neck and asked if I could see him now and wanted to know who I knew that had "the Sight". You knew all along, didn't you? That's why you wouldn't go after him for hurting me. He said he's going to blind me!'

'What on earth are you talking about?' asked Granny.

'Don't you get it? That boy is a faerie, and Granda knew all along. That's why he gave me this cross.'

Granny glared at Granda. 'This is what happens when you fill the child's head up with foolish stories right before bedtime.'

'I was not dreaming this! And we've got to help Stephen.'

'Maddy, it is four in the morning. You were having a bad dream. Now will you please go back to bed and let us all get some sleep!' said Granny.

'Oh sod this!' Maddy shoved past her granda and ran for the front door.

'Maddy, what has got into you?' said Granny as she tried to pull Maddy away from the bolts that secured the door at night.

'I'm getting him back before it's too late!' yelled Maddy, twisting in Granny's grip. 'Let go of me!'

Granda cleared his throat. 'Maybe I should go next door and check everything is OK? It's not normal for the dog to react like that.'

'Oh yes, listen to the dog!' said Maddy. 'What am I, invisible? You need Lassie to back up everything I say?'

'Maddy, will you stop being so dramatic?' said Granny. Then she turned to glare at her husband. 'Have you gone mad? You can't be waking people up this time of the night because a child and a dog are upset. Maddy had a bad dream, that's all. And that smelly devil of an animal shouldn't have been in here in the first place!'

'Still, I'm going to check,' muttered Granda. 'I'll sleep better if I know everything is all right.' He slipped his feet into the shoes he always left by his armchair, pulled his overcoat on over his pyjamas and unlocked the front door.

'You'll have the neighbours looking sideways at us, getting people out of their beds in the middle of the night over a child's nightmare,' Granny called after him.

Maddy was relieved someone was finally listening to her, but, to her horror, she started crying.

Granny sat on the bed and pulled her against her big soft chest and patted her back. 'You're getting yourself into a terrible state, Maddy. Once you know Stephen is safe and sound in his bed, will you go back to sleep?'

Maddy nodded, sick with misery and fear. She wished it was going to be that easy. She cringed inside as Granny kissed her cheek and cuddled her close, her stomach icy .

She heard Granda knock on the Forests' door. After what seemed like hours, Stephen's father opened the door, sounding sleepy and annoyed. Granda explained what Maddy had seen and asked if they could check.

'The children are fine, Bat. I think I'd know if someone was trying to get at them,' she heard Mr Forest say.

'Please check, Michael – the child's window is open and it's a cold night,' said Granda.

There was a moment of silence and then Maddy squeezed her eyes shut as Michael Forest's agonized shout tore at her heart. As Stephen's mother began to scream, her granny held her tighter, her old heart racing against Maddy's cheek.

'Sacred Heart, Maddy,' she whispered, her voice trembling. 'What on earth has happened?'

The cottage blazed with light and hummed with people. Stephen's three older brothers were huddled around the fire Granny had lit, while their mother sat in Granda's armchair. Mary Forest's face was red and swollen from crying and she curled into herself, rocking with anxiety. Granny was dressed and making endless cups of tea and sandwiches. Every now and then she would pause at the younger woman's chair to take a cold cup of tea from her hands, replace it with a fresh one and stroke her hair. Maddy could hear the crackle and squawk of police radios in the kitchen and outside their front door. All the people who lived around the square were awake now, the men getting ready to search for Stephen. Dawn was still some way off, but it was so busy it felt like the middle of the afternoon, even if everyone's face was tired and white beneath the electric lights. The old women who always seemed to circle like scavengers at weddings and funerals had turned up en masse, clutching their coal-scuttle handbags like weapons. They were sucking down tea and gossiping like crazy, swapping horror stories, oblivious to Stephen's mother.

The worst was being interviewed by the police in front of them all. Maddy watched lots of TV and was pretty sure she should have had a specially trained family-liaison officer and a bit of privacy, but what she got was fat old Sergeant O'Leary, who she was sure couldn't catch a cold. She tried to tell the truth, but once she started telling her story out loud in a room full of people who looked increasingly angry with her, she began to realize how it all sounded.

'I was in the Blarney Castle, walking the dog, when this boy came out of nowhere,' she said. 'He was a bit strange and then he grabbed me and said if I stopped struggling it would be a lot easier.'

'What did he mean by that?' said Sergeant O'Leary, writing in a notebook.

'He was trying to kidnap me,' said Maddy.

'Are you sure?'

'Well, I'm not a police officer, but I'm pretty confident that someone trying to drag you away against your will is abduction,' said Maddy.

'Maddy!' Granny barked a warning.

Maddy scowled while Sergeant O'Leary sighed and scribbled some more notes. 'And what did this boy look like?'

'About my height, skinny, really green eyes, red hair and freckles,' said Maddy.

'And you say he was the same boy who was outside your window just before Stephen Forest was discovered to have gone missing?'

'Well, yes . . .' said Maddy. 'But he didn't look the same.'

Sergeant O'Leary raised an eyebrow. 'Oh? How so?'

'Well . . .' Maddy was horrified to feel herself blushing, but she had to tell him. 'His face had gone all weird. He had, like, a snout, and his hands were really long and he had long tufty ears . . .' Her voice trailed off into silence as she realized how stupid she sounded.

Sergeant O'Leary looked down at his notes and sucked his teeth. 'Your granny says your granda was telling you faerie tales before bedtime.'

'Yeah, he was, but I know what I saw!' said Maddy, her voice sharp in anger. She bit her lip as Granny sent a look her way.

Sergeant O'Leary looked hard at her. 'Do you think you saw a faerie, Maddy?'

'Well . . . I don't know for sure,' she stammered. 'But people don't look like that, and that is what I saw. I was wide awake. I wasn't dreaming it.'

Sergeant O'Leary snapped the notebook shut. 'That will do for now, I think.' He pursed his lips as he tucked it away into his top pocket. 'You know, Maddy, we need to find Stephen quickly, and any false information we have been given will make our job a lot more difficult. You will think about that and come and tell me the minute you remember anything else, won't you?'

Maddy looked at the ground and nodded silently. As Granny let Sergeant O'Leary out, she could feel all the old women's eyes boring into her scalp. She felt so stupid. What she had seen didn't sound right, even to her. She sneaked a glance at Mrs Forest from the corner of her eye. She was glaring at Maddy.

'I'm so sorry, Liam,' she heard Granny saying. 'She got a terrible fright from that lad in the castle earlier, and all the stories Bat tells her . . . well, I think they got mixed up in her head with bad dreams. She's only a child.'

'Maybe so, Maureen, but she's old enough to know the difference between fantasy and reality. Telling me faerie stories when we are trying to find a missing child is not helping. She is wasting police time.'

Maddy snorted. All Sergeant O'Leary ever did was sit around on his big bum in the Garda station, stuffing his face. It was impossible to waste his time.

'I know, Liam. Let her get some sleep and I'll talk to her again in the morning.'

The door closed with a click and Maddy felt Granny's gnarled hands on her shoulders, guiding her up and into her bedroom. George's black and white face peered up from under her bed. Everyone had forgotten he was still in the house.

'Maddy, I want you to get some sleep and then we are going to talk to Sergeant O'Leary again,' said Granny. 'You need to have a good think about what you saw and get your head straight. This is no time to be messing.'

'I'm not!' said Maddy.

Granny sighed. 'I know you don't think you are, love, but honestly – a faerie? That's not what happened. You were half asleep and your dreams affected what you saw. You need to remember what really happened. For Stephen's sake.' She kissed her on the cheek before leaving the room.

Maddy lay on her bed and looked up at the ceiling. George jumped up and put his head on her chest, gazing at her with sad brown eyes. She heard Granny arguing in the kitchen with one of her friends, and she didn't need to hear what they were saying to know it was about her. She got up and crawled under the bed, her fingers feeling around in the dark until they brushed a cardboard box she had tucked into a corner.

She pulled it out and put it on the bed. She took a deep breath before lifting the lid. It was what her mother had called a 'sentimental' box, full of the priceless things that Maddy kept to remember the life she used to have.

Her mother had had a sentimental box on the top shelf of her wardrobe. She used to take it down sometimes, gently pick up everything inside and tell Maddy its story. The plastic bracelet that had been on Maddy's wrist in the hospital where she had been born; her first pair of shoes, fitting snugly into her palm; the candle in the shape of a number one that Maddy had blown out on her first birthday cake; the velvet wedding dress her mother had danced in all night.

Her mother's sentimental box, the photo albums and the jewellery Maddy had loved to stroke with a fingertip had been put away by her aunts, who told her she could have them when she grew up. So Maddy had started her own sentimental box with things she had salvaged in her aunties' wake as they had swept through her home. A book her mother had been reading, the bookmark Maddy had made for her at school still marking her place; a single earring she had found on the floor; the spare key ring of the car her father had been so proud of.

But the best thing in her box was a photo a stranger had taken of the three of them on a beach in Spain, the last holiday they had before the accident. Maddy sat between her parents with her arms wrapped tight around her knees, grinning into the camera, her tangled, salty hair blowing back from her face. Her father was smiling and looking down at her, while her mother was turning her face into her father's shoulder and laughing, her chestnut hair lifted off her shoulders by the sea breeze, the spreading strands shining red in the sun. They all looked so tanned and happy, elbows and thighs dusted with sand.

She sighed and looked around her room. Her grandparents had tried, but it really wasn't a child's room. Her double mahogany bed, ravaged by the effects of woodworm and sporting a lumpy mattress, matched the rest of the old-fashioned furniture. The wallpaper looked like wedding wrapping paper, and everything Maddy owned was in boxes under the bed. She didn't feel like this was home enough to ask her grandfather to put some shelves up. She knew her aunts thought she was too much for her elderly grandparents to cope with, and any day now the family might decide she had gone too far and she would be packed off to live in Cork city with one set of cousins and a frosty-faced matriarch. After what had just happened, there might not even be time to drill the holes.

Carefully she lifted a piece of black velvet from the box and unwrapped a cut crystal bottle, half full of pale gold perfume, her mother's favourite. She wet her pillow with two precious drops and slid the box back under the bed before pulling the pillow beneath her cheek, curling her body around George and crying herself to sleep.

CHAPTER five

It seemed like only a few minutes later that she felt herself being shaken awake.

'Maddy. Maddy, wake up,' Granny was saying.

The room was dark, and wind and rain were smashing against her window. Granny was grinning like someone had stuck a coat hanger in her mouth.

'What's the matter?' Maddy asked, almost dislocating her jaw with a huge yawn. George dipped his back and stretched his legs before jumping off the bed and padding out to the kitchen.

'It's Stephen – they found him!'

'Where?'

'In the castle grounds. Poor little fella was wandering about in his pyjamas crying for his mammy – not a mark on him, thank God.'

'Can I go and see him?'

'No darling, not yet. The doctor is taking a look at

him and then he needs to get some rest. You'll see him tomorrow.'

'What time is it?'

'It's eight o clock, but don't worry about getting up – I think after the night we have all had we could do with a day off.'

'Eight o'clock? So it took half the village four hours to find Stephen in the castle grounds? They're not that big.'

Granny rolled her eyes. 'They were looking in other places for him too, and he is a small child. Can you not just be grateful he's back, safe and sound?'

Maddy looked at Granny for a second and decided not to push it. There was someone better able to answer her questions. She heard the front door open.

'That will be your grandfather. Get up and I'll make us all a fry.'

Granda was stamping his feet on the Welcome mat and easing his rain-sodden coat off his shoulders when Maddy walked into the room. She waited until Granny had switched the radio on in the kitchen and the bacon and sausages had begun to sizzle before she spoke to him. She didn't want Granny to hear this conversation. Granda was stretching his long legs out in front of the fire, his tired head beginning to droop on to his chest.

Maddy sat in Granny's chair and said, 'I told the truth last night.'

He looked up at her warily, his eyes bloodshot from lack of sleep. 'Oh?'

'Yes – *everything*. About the way this boy looked, about what he *really* is, about how it all ties in with those stories you tell.'

He shifted in his chair and looked into the fire.

'No one believes me. You need to tell them I wasn't lying.'

He still didn't look at her. All he said was, 'You can't tell faerie tales to the police, Maddy. It's not right.'

He couldn't have hurt her more if he had slapped her in the face. She stared at him with her mouth open, her eyes filling with tears. He could have told everyone she wasn't a liar; he could have stuck up for her.

A tear spilled down her cheek, but she dashed it away with her palm. She glared at him and felt the welcome taste of molten anger ooze up from her belly. She got up and walked over to him. She leaned down and hissed in his ear, 'I'll tell you what isn't right. You knew what I met last night. You could have sorted him out. You could have stopped this happening to Stephen.'

He flinched, but he still would not meet her eye. Maddy stormed to her room and began to get dressed. She yanked her anorak on and banged her bedroom door behind her. She pulled the house keys off the hook so violently she almost yanked the wooden key holder from the wall.

'Where on earth are you going?' Granny was standing in the living room with her apron on and a spatula in her hand. 'Breakfast is going to be ready in ten minutes.'

'You can stuff your breakfast. I'm going to see Stephen.'

'Don't you dare speak to me like that, young lady. Get back here right now!'

Maddy slammed the door shut behind her so hard the windows rattled. It was only half a dozen steps from her grandparents' front door to the Forests' house, but it was raining so hard that her hair hung in rat's tails by the time she knocked on their door. Granny wrenched their front door open and hissed, 'Get back in here, *now*!' but Maddy glared at her and shook her head. Granny started to step outside but just then the Forests' front door opened and Maddy shot into their hallway.

The massive shape of Mr Forest loomed over her as he shut the door. Maddy cringed when she thought of how she must have sounded last night. Remembering the look on Mrs Forest's face she held her breath, waiting for his reaction, but his face split into a huge smile.

'Maddy love, have you come to see Stephen? That's good of you. He'll like that.'

Mrs Forest appeared out of the kitchen, still dressed

in the clothes she had worn the night before. Her face was tired but happy and she grabbed Maddy and gave her a huge hug that squeezed all the breath out of her.

'Maddy, thank you, thank you for being awake and seeing Stephen go off like that. What would we have done if you had been asleep?'

'Ummm—'

'The doctor is with him right now, but he won't be long. You can go to his room and see him then. Will you have a bite to eat while you're waiting?'

'Actually, I think Granny was making breakfast—'

'Ah, you will,' Mrs Forest carried on. 'Sure, a little bite to eat won't spoil your appetite for breakfast, a growing girl like you. You need all the help you can get.'

Mrs Forest herded Maddy through the sitting room to the kitchen at the back of the house. It was warm and bright and steam fogged up the windows. She bustled about making Maddy a ham sandwich and added a slice of jam sponge to the plate. *It's obviously never too early for cake*, thought Maddy. As Mrs Forest chattered away, she leaned over with a towel and gave Maddy's hair a quick rub to stop it dripping rainwater down her neck. Maddy was trying to eat the sandwich and she almost choked, but Mrs Forest talked on regardless.

'. . . not a scratch on him. He's a lucky little devil, wandering around the grounds with no shoes or socks on. It's funny because he's never sleepwalked before, but the doctor says it's a childhood thing and he should grow out of it. Imagine him opening his window fast asleep, though, and just climbing out! I've never seen him do that wide awake . . .'

Maddy listened, a cold feeling settling in the pit of her stomach. The bread turned dry and lumpy in her mouth. *Sleepwalking?* she thought. *They think Stephen was sleepwalking?*

'What about the boy who was outside the window last night?' she asked.

'Oh sure, Maddy, you were doing a bit of sleepwalking yourself last night. You just got your dreams mixed up, that's all.' Mrs Forest laughed. 'Faeries indeed! Your granda is going to have a hard time living that one down in the pub.'

She heard heavy footsteps in the hall and the sound of men's voices. 'That'll be the doctor,' said Mrs Forest, before rushing out to talk to him. As the doctor and Stephen's parents stood by the front door, Maddy quietly eased herself up from her chair and slipped into the little boy's room.

She pushed the door back, not knowing what to expect, and let out a sigh of relief when she saw Stephen's little figure sitting up in his bed. The rain poured down the window and it made the blue walls look as if they were underwater, as the patterns of the storm played over every surface.

'Stephen?' she whispered. He didn't look up. She walked into the room and sat on the end of his bed.

'Stephen, are you OK?'

He looked up at her then, and Maddy caught her breath at the sight of him. His face was thin and white, his eyes dark holes sunken into his head. His hands were little blind spiders that plucked at his duvet, so pale that every vein stood out a cold blue. It was weird. It was like he was . . . fading. *He's just tired*, thought Maddy.

'It's OK, you know, I saw it all,' said Maddy. 'I know you weren't sleepwalking. You can tell me what happened.'

The hands stopped their plucking then. Somewhere in the depths of his eyes were two pinpricks of light that focused on her face. He was listening to her now.

'Say something, will you?' Maddy offered him a little smile. 'You're beginning to freak me out here.'

The hands began to pluck again and the little lights in his eyes shifted away into blackness. The smile died on Maddy's face. This just wasn't like Stephen.

She leaned forward to touch his hand, and as she did so the iron cross that hung around her neck slipped loose from her V-necked T-shirt and swung in front of Stephen's eyes. Maddy watched in horror as his face crumpled in on itself. He opened his mouth wide and hissed at her, baring sharp yellow teeth. She froze and felt her skin go into goosebumps all over her body. She slid back cautiously. The creature in the bed began to pluck at the duvet again.

'You're not Stephen, are you?'

The lights flickered in its eyes as the creature in Stephen's bed, wearing Stephen's favourite dinosaur pyjamas, looked straight at her. Then it began to laugh, a dry, rasping wheeze that would have sounded more at home in a graveyard than in the chest of a two-year-old. The wind outside whined in sympathy.

Maddy tried to look calm, but her legs shook as she got up and walked backwards toward the door. She felt for the cool brass knob, keeping her eyes on the creature. Her body hummed with tension as she imagined it leaping for her, ready to sink those yellow teeth into her throat. But its eyes were dull again and it stared listlessly out the window.

'Don't get too comfortable, pal. You're not staying,' she whispered, as she wrenched the door open and bolted into the hallway, slamming it shut behind her.

Maddy almost ran out of the house, eager to be gone before any of Stephen's family stopped her. She didn't think she could talk to them right now, not until she figured out what was going on. But Stephen's father poked his head around the kitchen door as she reached for the door handle.

'Are you off already, Maddy?'

'Yeah, umm, I think Stephen is a bit tired ... probably best if I come back later,' she said.

'OK, we'll see you soon.'

She was letting herself out when she thought of something and turned back to him.

'Mr Forest, you worked on the faerie kingdom in the castle grounds, didn't you?' she asked.

'Yes. I've heard how much you like playing in there,' he said with a wink. 'That was some time ago now – it's held up well over the years.'

'Did local people make all the stuff that's in there?'

'Some of it. Some of it was already there.'

'What about the faerie mound?'

'No, no, that was already there. The grounds around the castle used to be stuffed with things like that,' said Mr Forest. 'Some even say there's a barrow of an ancient king, stuffed with treasure. They're always chucking out tourists with metal detectors, trying to dig the place up. But I believe that as much as I believe in the ghosts that haunt the castle.'

'So no one created that mound with a JCB then?'

'No, we just put a sign on it and the gardeners tidied

it up a bit. Saved us a few days' work, I can tell you. Why do you ask?'

'No reason.' Maddy smiled at him. 'Tell Stephen I'll be coming back for him very, very soon.'

He looked puzzled – perhaps she'd overdone the threatening tone – but smiled a goodbye as she closed the door.

Maddy stood on the Forests' doorstep with her head tipped back and tried to stare at the raindrops as they hurtled toward her eyeballs. She thought of the creature in the house, and that familiar, comforting feel of anger on the boil began to swirl lazily in her stomach.

I'm getting Stephen back if it kills me, she thought.

CHAPTER SIX

Granny was waiting for Maddy when she walked back in. Her coat was buttoned up to throat, her sensible walking shoes were on her feet and her black leather handbag hung from one wrist. She looked armoured up and murderous. She didn't wait for Maddy to try to say sorry.

'I will not be spoken to like that, young lady,' she snapped, her fingers whitening as they bit down on her black leather gloves. 'I don't deserve to be treated in such a disgusting way by you – have you anything to say for yourself?'

Maddy lidded her eyes and leaned against the door jamb. 'Sorry.'

'That doesn't sound very sincere.'

Maddy shrugged. Granny clenched her jaw in anger but Maddy thought her eyes were a bit watery. Shame pricked her skin, but she looked away.

'Are you at least going to tell me what's got you so riled up?'

'Why don't you ask *him*?' Maddy pointed at Granda with her chin. He was sitting in his armchair, buried behind the local paper.

'Are *you* going to tell me what's going on?' Granny snapped at him.

He just grunted and rattled the pages as he turned them.

Granny took a deep breath. 'Right then. It's Halloween tomorrow and we've got visitors coming. I'm going to do the shopping, and when I get back the two of you had better have sorted this out.'

Maddy squeezed up against the TV table as her grandmother reached past her to open the door. Her eyes really were full of tears, big fat ones that huddled against the red rims of her eyes, waiting to overflow and streak her powdered cheeks.

'I know you're angry, love,' Granny whispered, 'but you're not the only one who's hurting.'

Maddy looked down at her feet, a lump rising in her throat. But then the anger woke up and poked a finger in her ribs. *I lost everything*, she thought resentfully. *Parents, school, friends – my whole life. What does she know? And now, thanks to Granda, my life here isn't going to be worth living.*

She could feel Granny's eyes on her, but she didn't trust herself to look up in case she started crying.

That had happened before and it just got so messy and embarrassing. Granny placed a hand against her cheek and waited a moment. Maddy kept staring at her scruffy trainers and she felt Granny's sigh sweep over the crown of her head before she stepped out the door, closing it gently behind her.

Maddy stayed where she was, waiting for Granda to say something. The ticking clock boomed in the tense quiet while the fire snapped and growled. He just carried on reading the paper.

Eventually Maddy stomped into her bedroom and pulled a box of books out from under her bed. She had loved myths, legends and faerie tales when she was little, and her parents had bought her loads of books about faeries. She dug around until she found a collection of Irish myths and folklore, then flicked through the pages until she found what she was looking for – stolen human children and changelings.

There he was. Sean Rua, Red John. He had said his name was John. A wicked sprite who masqueraded as a boy and carried off children.

She walked back into the living room with the book held open in her hand. She put its spine on the top of Granda's paper and shoved down as hard as she could, tearing the newspaper from his fingers and leaving it a crumpled heap in his lap.

'What's got into you?' he yelled, his face going red.

She glared back at him and tapped the page of the book with her finger.

'Read that.'

He glanced down at the book and the red leaked out of his face. But then he shoved it off his lap and started trying to smooth the pages of his paper flat. Maddy clenched her teeth to try to keep her temper.

'Are you not even going to ask me why I want you to read that page?' she asked.

'I don't have time to play games with you, Maddy,' he growled. 'I'm tired. I've been up half the night looking for Stephen.'

'It's a shame you didn't find him then,' she said.

He went very, very still when she said that. She cocked her head to one side and watched him. He looked uncomfortable and stared into the fire. Maddy sat in Granny's chair and waited for him to say something. The silence stretched out between them.

'You know that isn't Stephen next door, don't you? You also know why that faerie asked me if I could see him now. He's threatened to blind me – do you know that?'

He flinched, but he still didn't speak.

'I need to know what's going on,' said Maddy. 'He might come back.'

Granda sighed then and pinched the bridge of his nose. 'Just wear the cross and keep away from the mound.'

'You need to tell me why I should even listen to you.'

He glared at her. 'Because you have the Sight, Maddy. It makes you special. It means you can See faerie folk, and they don't take too kindly to it.'

'What will they do?'

'They will either try to blind you or, if you have a special talent, they take you as a pet. Neither of them is a nice option. You need to stay safe.'

'This is rubbish,' said Maddy. 'If I've got the Sight, how come I didn't See faeries before?'

'You did, when you were a baby. Your mother had the Sight and she learned to stay out of their way, but when you were born and she saw you reaching out to them whenever you were outside, she decided to take you and your father away,' he said. 'That's why she went to London. Faeries can't live in cities; they can't stand all the iron.'

'I don't remember Seeing faeries before.'

'Your mind has taught you not to see things you are convinced do not exist. That fright you got the other night and my telling you the rules must have opened it up a crack.' He smiled thinly. 'It's nice to see something gets through to you.'

'Can you See them?'

'Yes. It runs in the family. But I pretend not to See them. I wear iron –' he lifted his shirtsleeve to show her a dull cuff on his wrist – 'and I stay home when the sun goes down, as much as I can. They're stronger when the light fades.'

'Can Granny See?'

'No! And I don't want you to upset her either, talking about what you can See. The Unsighted in this world are better off not knowing about these things.'

'You knew that thing wasn't Stephen when you found it, didn't you?'

He looked ashamed, but he nodded.

'What is it?'

'A faerie changeling,' said Granda, looking faintly sick. 'One of their own that is weak and ill. They take human children and put them in their place. They don't like dealing with their own problems too much.'

'What do they do with the human children?'

'Who knows?' said Granda. 'They keep them as servants, pets . . . No one knows for sure.'

'How many people in the village have the Sight?' asked Maddy.

Granda looked at her warily. 'A few. Dr Malloy for one; Sheila who works at the castle gift shop . . . there's about twenty of us, I'd say.' He smiled at her sadly.

'Enough for a rescue party,' said Maddy. 'When you go after Stephen, I'm coming with you.'

'Rescue party . . . ?!' Granda looked at her, surprise widening his eyes. He put a hand on her shoulder. 'Stephen is gone, love.'

She stared at him in horror, and then her eyes hardened with anger. 'We're getting him back, or else I go next door and I tell Mr and Mrs Forest exactly what's going on.'

'What are you going to tell them, Maddy? That he's not their son? That they've got a faerie changeling in the house? They won't believe you, and even if they did, it wouldn't do them any good to know the truth. Stephen is gone. Let them be happy with what they think is their son – you're only going to break their hearts.'

'But they'll know!'

'They won't. They'll only see what they want to see. They might think he acts strange, that he doesn't thrive the way he should, but they will learn to live with it.'

'But what about Stephen?'

'I told you, Maddy, he's gone. Stolen children go into the mound and we can't follow.'

'Why not?'

'Because we can't. We wouldn't last five minutes in their world. You can't fight anyone as old and powerful as the Tuatha de Dannan and the other faeries.'

'Who are the Tuatha de Dannan?'

'The old ones, the Shining Ones, the Gentry, the ones we tell stories about that you laugh at. We call them faeries now, but we used to call them gods when they ruled Ireland a long, long time ago. Faeries like Sean Rua are bad enough, but they are nothing compared to the Tuatha de Dannan, and they are the ones who rule Tír na nÓg. I'm telling you, Maddy, it can't be done. It's why your mother took you away. She didn't want you to be one of the stolen ones. Go after Stephen and you'll be starting a fight we can't win, and God knows how many people will suffer then. We've lived with the faeries this long because we've learned to protect ourselves from them and make sure we don't cross paths with them too often. Draw the attention of the Tuatha, and nobody is safe. I'm fond of Stephen, but I won't risk you or your grandmother for him. And his father would say the same, if it was you that was missing.'

Maddy leaned forward and put her head in her hands. She stretched the skin on her face with her palms while she stared at the floor. She couldn't believe this. Faeries existed, they had stolen Stephen, and Granda, her strong, sort-anything-out Granda, was just going to sit by the fire and hope the faeries didn't notice him.

She got up and walked to the window to watch the

rain. It hadn't stopped since Stephen went missing. It was lighter now, constant soft rain, as if the leaden sky was weeping. The dark clouds were spreading out from Blarney Castle, stretching long black fingers toward the village. As she watched, the clouds became slightly thicker and blacker and spread their shadow a little further, but the rain never got any worse. There were no dogs barking, the birds roosted miserably with their sodden feathers fluffed into balls, while the saplings were bending almost to the ground under the weight of water.

'Was it like this before, when the others went missing?' she asked.

'What?'

'The weather.'

Granda looked at the window, then he got up and steered her away by the shoulders.

'No, this is different,' he said, his face grim. 'But the Samhain Fesh is almost upon us, when they are at their strongest. It will be over soon, and then we can all get back to normal.'

'Except for Stephen, of course,' she snapped. She shrugged his hands off her shoulders, furious at his weakness, at how little he seemed to care.

'Maddy, you have to let this go. It will send you mad otherwise.'

'No, I won't! You're actually just going to leave him? Would you leave me if they took me?'

His jaw dropped and she could tell she had scored a point.

'Of course not! I look after my own, because it's all I can do,' he shouted. 'I thank God it isn't you and I look away, like plenty of others have done in this village.'

'How many times has this happened exactly?' asked Maddy, her voice shaking with shock and anger. 'How many other children have you Sighted let go into the mound and done nothing to help?'

'That's enough now, Maddy,' he said. 'There's nothing more to talk about.'

'No, because you should be *doing* something!' she yelled.

'WHAT CAN I DO?' Granda shouted back. 'Do you want me to go marching into the Garda station and start telling them faerie stories? What do you think will happen then, Maddy? Do you think they'll say, "Oh, right so, now that you've told us, we'll just go and swap the changeling for Stephen and arrest any faeries that come back into Blarney."? They will think I'm mad, Maddy, an old man who's gone soft in the head. There's plenty of Sighted sitting in mental hospitals who will never be free again because they tried to tell people about the faeries, and that's not going to be me. Because what do you think will happen to your granny if the faeries find out I've tried to tell people about them? She can't even see them coming, Maddy. I have to keep my own family safe. There's nothing I can do for Stephen now.'

Anger flooded Maddy's head and pressed against her eyeballs. It turned her breath so hot it scorched her lips as she glared at him. 'I'm not going to drop this,' she said.

'Yes, you are,' said Granda.

'You need to stick up for your friends,' said Maddy. 'You taught me that.'

Granda looked back at her, his bloodshot eyes wet with unshed tears. 'There are some fights, Maddy, you have to walk away from.'

She shook her head slowly. 'No, you're wrong. If I let Stephen go, that'll be just as bad as you and everyone else in this village who has turned a blind eye for years,' she said. 'I couldn't live with myself.'

CHAPTER SEVEN

Maddy sulked and stomped about the house all day, refusing to speak to either of her grandparents. Come bedtime, George was banished to his kennel, despite the rain, while Maddy sneaked a torch into her bedroom so she could scour her books for information on faeries when she was supposed to be asleep. But all her books described was sweet tiny things that granted wishes, not ones taller than her that went bump in the night. When she finally fell into an exhausted sleep, the sound of the rain drumming on the roof was the last thing she heard.

It was also the sound that greeted her the next morning. The wind sighed and wept in a soft way that was beginning to get on Maddy's nerves. It was as if the weather was going out of its way to be atmospheric and mystical. If the faeries were behind this, then they had really tacky taste.

'You're overdoing things, folks,' she said aloud in her bedroom.

It was Sunday, Halloween, and it was her job to fetch the papers from the local shop. She got dressed quickly and grabbed the change that had been left for her on the TV table. On the way she stopped by the village payphone and called her cousin Roisin. Her Aunt Fionnula sounded frosty when she answered the phone, but Maddy didn't have time to work out what she had done to upset her this time.

'Hello?' said Roisin, her mouth full as usual. Granny said Roisin was 'sensitive'. It meant she ate a lot for comfort.

'Hey. Roisin, it's Maddy. How's it going? I need you to go online, google faeries – f-a-e-r-i-e-s – and find out everything you can about fighting them and getting into a faerie mound.'

'Good morning to you too, Maddy. Why should I be doing this for you?' said Roisin.

'It's for a project we're doing at school. I'm going to get in deep trouble if I don't get it done. I should have done it over the holidays, but there's nothing in the library and we haven't got the Internet,' said Maddy. Her grandparents hadn't got a mobile phone yet, never mind a computer.

'I can't keep doing your homework, Maddy. I'll get in big trouble if Mam catches me,' said Roisin.

Maddy gritted her teeth. 'I don't want you to write the essay – I want you to get *me* the information so *I* can write the essay,' said Maddy. 'I just want you to print off a few pages for me and bring them round when you come.' She knew her relatives would be paying their regular Sunday duty visit.

'I don't know, Maddy. Dad doesn't really like us printing stuff off. He says the ink costs a fortune, he'll go mad—'

'Please, Roisin, *please*!' interrupted Maddy. 'I wouldn't ask if I wasn't really desperate. Honestly, Roisin, I never ask for anything. Can you not do me a favour this once?'

Roisin hesitated. 'You *do* ask for favours, you know . . . oh, fine, OK, but I'm not printing anything off for you ever again. You *have* to persuade Granny and Granda to get a computer. Hey, are you dressing up for Halloween?'

Maddy hung up on her. She glanced at the sky as she hurried to the local supermarket. The clouds were right overhead now, looking as if they were about to reach down and grab her in their sooty fingers.

Later, after Mass, Maddy played the good girl by offering to run errands for her grandparents so they could sit by the fire and keep out of the wet. Luckily for her, one of them involved bringing the local paper round to an elderly neighbour. The old lady asked her in for a biscuit and while she rummaged in the kitchen Maddy managed to steal her poker. She was back home just before lunch, putting it in her rucksack to join the one she had already stolen from her grandparents and hiding the bag behind the coal shed, when Roisin came hurrying down the path.

'Quick, take these off me before Dad sees them,' she said, as she pulled sheets of paper out of her jacket. Maddy rolled them up without looking at them and stuffed them inside the bag.

'What did you find out?'

'Old wives' tales, stuff about them not liking iron, that sort of thing,' said Roisin.

'Anything about getting into a faerie mound?' asked Maddy.

Roisin frowned. 'Not much – it was a very specific request. I did find one entry, but it was a bit strange . . .'

'Maddy!'

Roisin and Maddy froze as they heard the braying voice of Danny, the Asbo-in-waiting. He was waiting for them as they came out from behind the shed, practically dancing with joy. Maddy groaned inwardly. If he was happy, then she was in big, big trouble. She ran through all her recent memories to try to figure out the cause and what she could do about it.

'Oooh, Maddy, you're for it. Mum is HOPPING and she wants to talk to you right now!'

Maddy felt her insides churn. Of all her aunts,

Fionnula was the worst. A grim, unsmiling woman, her entrance into a room made water boil and flowers wilt. Luckily you could always hear her coming, as she wore nothing but nylon tracksuits, in pastel colours. The soft hiss of her thighs rubbing together was enough warning for children and animals to flee.

Aunt Fionnula was in the living room with Granny and Granda, waiting for Maddy. She was standing with her back to the fire and her arms folded. Her brood huddled on the sidelines – she liked an audience when she was humiliating someone. It always amazed Maddy that someone who so clearly did not like children had had so many of them. Aunt Fionnula was all square, hard lines, from her letter box of a mouth to the shape of her face. Even her dark hair was sprayed stiff into a helmet that a sun-blinded sparrow could bounce off. The only thing that looked soft about her was her shell suits – she was wearing a green one today. The shiny material reflected back on to her face and made her look queasy.

Aunt Fionnula was a firm believer in duty, discipline and the medicinal qualities of cod liver oil. Her children did not talk back or make a mess and they got good grades in school. She declared to anyone who would listen that the fact that Maddy achieved the opposite was evidence that the child needed a *firm hand* and that it was her moral duty to take her dead sister's daughter away from her elderly parents and give Maddy the discipline and boundaries she was so clearly crying out for. Aunt Fionnula would have been surprised to learn that Maddy too was a fervent believer in boundaries. She would dearly like there to be one between herself and Aunt Fionnula that was three metres high, spiked on top and guarded by men with machine guns.

'You've been telling lies again,' snapped Aunt Fionnula.

Maddy stood by the door to the kitchen and glared at her. Her grandparents sat in their chairs either side of her aunt. Granny had obviously been crying. Granda just looked very tired. What on *earth* had she done? If it was this bad, why couldn't she remember?

'Well, what have you got to say for yourself, young lady?' demanded Aunt Fionnula.

'You haven't told me what I'm supposed to have done yet,' she said.

Aunt Fionnula looked happy, which meant Maddy had just shot herself in the foot. 'Oh, it's not what you are *supposed* to have done, Maddy, it's what you *have* done,' she said. 'Mrs Mackie heard you the other day, and she told me she was shocked to hear a child so brazen. In the shop, trying to jump the queue, telling people you needed to get out quickly because your parents were waiting for you in the car.'

Maddy had forgotten about that. It seemed such a small lie. Trust Mrs Mackie to hear her and go running off to tell tales to this shiny, stiff, grim-faced hag.

'Leave the poor child alone, Fionnula. This not doing anyone any good,' said Granda.

'We have to put a stop to this, Da,' Fionnula snapped.

She turned back to Maddy. 'Why do you do it? Why do you tell people your parents are still alive?' she demanded.

Maddy stood there, staring at her. Her body prickled all over with fear and embarrassment. *Isn't it obvious?* she felt like screaming. *Isn't it bloody obvious?*

There was a tiny sound in the room, a rush of air. Maddy looked at Roisin, who was going as red as a tomato. The sound had been her intake of breath as she opened her mouth to speak, but she froze in her mother's gimlet stare.

'Have you something to say, young lady?' snapped Aunt Fionnula.

'Um, well . . . just . . . you know . . . it's not that bad. Is it?' Roisin offered in a voice that got smaller and smaller.

'*What* isn't?' asked Aunt Fionnula in a voice that dripped pure acid.

'Er, what she said?' said Roisin.

'Clearly you and I don't agree on what is acceptable behaviour,' hissed Aunt Fionnula. 'Be quiet. I will talk to *you* later.'

Roisin shrank back against the wall and looked at her feet, her face practically throbbing from the heat of her blush.

Aunt Fionnula turned back to Maddy. 'I'm still waiting for my answer. And my patience is wearing thin.'

Maddy glared back at her aunt and shrugged her shoulders. Aunt Fionnula's eyes bulged in her head and then she ran at Maddy, grabbing her by the shoulders and shaking her.

'Why do you do it? Are you trying to upset us all?' she screamed, red in the face, spit flying off her yellow teeth. 'Is it not bad enough your mother and father are gone, without your telling lies about them? How can my mother bear to have you in her house when you say things like that?'

'Get off me!' Maddy shoved her aunt in the chest to break her grip and then swung her hand, hard, and clocked her a good one right in the face. In the shocked silence Maddy could see the imprint of her fingers start to glow on her aunt's white cheek. All the anger drained out of her and fear turned her legs to water. *I've done it now*, she thought.

'What *are* you doing, Fionnula?' asked Granny, her voice shaking. 'She's just a child. What harm is she doing if she wants to pretend her mother and father are still alive?'

Aunt Fionnula's eyes bulged with anger. 'How

can you take her side? She can't say such vicious things!'

Granny shook her head sadly. 'How was it vicious? Can you not understand why a ten-year-old who has lost her parents would say something like that? You're a mother yourself.'

'I think you've made your feelings clear, Fionnula. Let it go now,' said Granda. He stood and put his arm around Maddy's shoulders as Aunt Fionnula glared at her, her palm to her face. Her free hand shook as she pointed a finger at Maddy, but her voice was icy and steady.

'Don't you see how bad she is? She's *violent,* and you don't say a word. There are lines that should not be crossed, and that child has gone too far, too often,' she said. 'I know you try your best with her, but you shouldn't be trying to raise a ten-year-old at your time of life, especially not a *difficult* one. You are not doing the best thing for Maddy either – she's running wild. She's got the whole village talking about how she made up all that stuff when Stephen went missing, just so she could get attention. It has to stop. She *hit* me, for goodness sake.'

Granda looked at Aunt Fionnula, his face unreadable. 'She certainly did.'

Aunt Fionnula took a deep breath. 'Face it – you cannot cope with her,' she said to her parents in a softer tone of voice. *You snake*, thought Maddy. 'It's best that

Maddy come and live with me, where she can have the company of other children and the kind of environment she needs.'

Granny sighed and stood up. 'We've had this out before and I'm not talking about it any more,' she said. 'I know you are grieving too, Fionnula, but you need to take a long, hard look at yourself and ask if you really are the person who should be looking after Maddy. Come and help me get the lunch ready, Roisin,' she said. Roisin threw a guilty, embarrassed look at Maddy, even as she scrambled to get out of the room.

'Perhaps I didn't handle things well today,' said Fionnula to Granda, smoothing her shell suit over her thunder thighs. Her face was still red and her eyes were flinty so Maddy was under no illusion that her aunt was having a change of heart. 'But I still think, for Maddy's sake, we need to make a decision soon,' she went on. 'I know you feel you owe it to her mother, but no one can say you haven't tried. It is time for someone younger to take over. And mark my words,' she hissed as she glared at Maddy, 'there will be no lies told or any backchat once I get my hands on you. You will do things my way. A month with me and you will be a different child.'

A week and I'll burn the house down, thought Maddy. *That hair would flare up a treat.*

CHAPTER EIGHT

Maddy went quickly to her room and shut the door so no one would see the hot tears coursing down her face. Granny knocked on the door to tell her lunch was ready, but Maddy said she didn't feel well. 'Do you want me to bring your lunch into you on a tray, pet?' Granny asked.

Maddy sighed and put her forehead against the door. 'I'll be OK in a little while. I'll eat then.'

She waited for Granny to open the door and argue with her, but instead she whispered, 'It's fine, love. You can have it a bit later.'

'Let her starve,' she heard Aunt Fionnula saying. 'She's only looking for attention.'

There was no way she was eating with Aunt Fionnula, much less living with her. *I hope she chokes*, thought Maddy. She sat on her bed, listening to the clink of cutlery and her aunt's harsh voice. Aunt Fionnula seemed to be the only one talking. Maddy picked at a loose thread on her duvet cover and thought about the 'environment' her aunt would provide for her: sharing a cold, damp box room with Roisin and forced to be her aunt's charity case. There would be no cuddles, no kisses, and no pet dog. Maddy would be forever on the sidelines, taught to *know her place*.

After lunch, Aunt Fionnula walked into Maddy's room without knocking, pushing a reluctant Roisin before her. 'We're off home, but Roisin is going to stay the night,' she trilled. 'You girls will be a sharing a room soon enough – you might as well get to know each other better.'

'I'm going to do a little bit of shopping in the village, while the boys play football in the square,' she went on. 'If you need anything, Roisin, give me a call on the mobile before I head home. Be a good girl for your grandparents.' She bent to give Roisin a quick peck on the cheek and then straightened up, casting a cold eye around Maddy's messy room, the boxes of books and toys spilling out from under the bed. 'You'll have to get rid of some of this clutter before you come to us, Maddy. We really don't have the room for it. I'm sure you don't need it all anyway.'

Maddy said nothing.

'Well then, girls,' said Aunt Fionnula with a brittle

smile, 'I'll see you both tomorrow, bright and early for school.'

Roisin looked at Maddy, who looked at the wall. Roisin sighed and picked up a book from the window ledge and started to leaf through it. Maddy waited. Eventually a peaceful hush fell over the house. She crept to the door and peeped around it. Both her grandparents were asleep in their chairs in front of the fire. She took her jacket from its hook on the back of her bedroom door and tiptoed past them into the kitchen. Roisin followed her and stared as Maddy flew around the room, grabbing fruit and a packet of biscuits and throwing them into a plastic bag before she started to make some jam sandwiches.

'What are you doing?'

Maddy refused to look at her. 'None of your business.' She threw the sandwiches into the bag with the rest of the food, zipped up her jacket and rummaged under the sink for a torch. Then she looked at her cousin. 'You didn't tell me earlier – about how you get into a faerie mound,' she said.

'What?'

Maddy widened her eyes impatiently and waited.

Roisin frowned and thought for a second. 'It was just one entry and it was a bit creepy. Only a faerie can open the mound; anyone else needs a guide.'

'And how do I get the guide?' said Maddy.

'You have to call them. If you want to get in, you have to give them something they value,' said Roisin.

'What?'

'The blood of an innocent.'

Maddy stared at her. 'You're joking.'

Roisin shrugged her shoulders helplessly. 'That's what it said. Why do you want to know this stuff anyway?'

Maddy sighed and walked over to the cutlery drawer, taking out a sharp paring knife and adding it to the bag. She took George's lead from its nail by the door, slipped the back-door key from beneath a china shepherdess posing on the kitchen shelf and let herself out.

She went behind the coal shed and picked up her rucksack, throwing the food in with the poker. Then she walked around to the shed door and pulled the bolts back before ducking inside. Coal dust drifted up her nose and made it itch. She began to rummage around for anything that could intimidate a faerie. She took down an old horseshoe her grandfather had hanging up for luck and slung it in the bag, then grabbed a handful of iron filings, stuffed them in her jacket pocket and zipped it up.

She jumped out of her skin when she turned around and nearly fell over Roisin.

'Will you go away!' she hissed.

'Tell me what you're doing,' said her cousin.

Maddy shoved past her and went to pull a sleepy George out of his kennel, before clipping the lead on to his collar and yanking the stiff gate open.

'Wait!' said Roisin, running to keep up.

'Go home!' said Maddy over her shoulder.

Maddy walked around the house and out into the lane, heading straight toward Blarney Castle. The sun was sinking, lost behind the fingers of black cloud, and the tarmac on the wet road shone like a mirror every time car headlights swept over it. Maddy was cold and her jeans were already wet. They felt like clammy cardboard tubes and they were chafing the skin on her thighs. She was going to look like corned beef if she didn't dry out soon. George wanted to stop at every street light and power-line pole to cock his leg, and Maddy had to keep yanking on the lead. The little terrier huffed in temper and tried to dig his paws in, but she pulled him along anyway. She knew she wasn't being fair, but she was in no mood to humour him. George's stubby legs worked hard to keep up with her, and drops of rain glittered in his whiskers. The rain had forced most of the village indoors. The bonfire for tonight loomed in the village square, too wet to be lit now, Maddy supposed. A little gang of early trick-or-treaters passed her by, heads bent, voices low, the rain beating them around their hoods.

Maddy swore when she heard Roisin running to catch her.

'Maddy, would you just stop for a second and tell me what is going on?'

'What's the point? I tell lies, remember? How will you know if I'm telling you the truth?'

'Maddy, you can't blame Mam – you did lie,' protested Roisin. 'You can't get out of it like you normally do. You can't be angry at Mam for being upset. Your mam was her sister.'

Maddy gritted her teeth and kept walking.

Roisin stopped dead in the lane. 'Maddy, please, if you don't tell me what's going on, I am going to have to call Mam on her mobile. Everyone is going to wonder where we are if I don't.'

'Why do you have to be such a pain, Roisin?' said Maddy. 'I didn't ask you to come, and I'm telling you: you're not going to believe me.'

'Tell me anyway,' said Roisin.

'OK, fine.' Maddy walked back and glared at her cousin. 'The night I went into the castle grounds I think I met a very nasty faerie who likes to take children. I think he took Stephen, and I'm going into the faerie mound to get Stephen back. Does that clear things up for you?'

Roisin stared at her with her mouth open and then she started to giggle.

'I said you wouldn't believe me,' said Maddy as she turned away and started to walk on.

'Well, you have to try a bit harder than that,' said Roisin, chasing after her again. 'Stephen is fine – everyone knows that.'

'You reckon? Go away, Ro.'

'Seriously, Maddy, where are you going?'

'Seriously, Ro, into the castle grounds, where it's dark and spooky, and I'm not going to turn back because you feel scared and start crying like a baby.'

Roisin's eyes started to sparkle. 'This is a Halloween trick, isn't it? Oh, let me come with you, pleeeease?'

'I tell you what,' said Maddy. 'Give me the phone so I know you can't call your mum, and then you can come with me.'

'Noooo,' said Roisin. 'Why don't I keep the phone, so you can't ditch me and go off on your own?'

'Fine.' Maddy sighed. 'Just shut up.'

It was almost dark and the car park was deserted. Maddy kept to the wall and the shadows where no grown-ups could see them. She hunkered down behind a bush, waiting for the gates to be locked. Roisin crouched next to her and thought for a couple of minutes.

'How are you going to get in?'

'There's a gap in the fence I can squeeze through. I used it last time.'

'No, I mean the faerie mound – how are you going to get into that?'

'Blood of an innocent, right?'

'Yeah?'

Maddy nodded at George. Even soaking wet and sitting on cold hard ground, the dog had a look of vacant happiness on his face. He put a paw on Maddy's knee and gave her face a lick.

'You can't use George!' screamed Roisin. Maddy shushed her urgently and Roisin lowered her voice. 'You can't use the dog!' she whispered.

'Why not? You can't get more innocent than George.'

'You're serious about trying to get into the mound? What makes you think it will work?'

'It's Halloween,' said Maddy. 'It's meant to be the time where the human and the faerie world open up to each other.'

'If you really want to try this, why don't you use your own blood?'

'Because if I believe everything your mother says about me, it would probably lock me out,' hissed Maddy.

Roisin bit her lip and looked at her trainers. They sat in gloomy silence, Maddy shifting her weight from one bum cheek to the other as the rain dripped off her hood.

Roisin stole a glance at Maddy's face. 'It won't be so bad, living with us.'

'Yes, it will. Now, please, *shut up*.'

After what seemed like an age they saw the light on the groundsman's bike as he finished checking for any stragglers. They heard the clink of metal on metal as he locked up and the sound of him whistling as he cycled off into the night. Maddy stood up and worked her way along behind the dripping bushes ringing the fence, feeling with her foot for the hole.

She scrambled through, tugging a reluctant George after her, and walked up the path, not bothering to see if Roisin was keeping up. It was pitch black under the trees and Maddy jumped every time she heard a strange noise or a rustle in the undergrowth. The trees seemed to be shuddering with moving shapes and twice she thought she heard giggling. She shivered but she didn't dare put the torch on until they had crossed the bridge and were far enough away from the car park that any adults would not see the light. The grounds, landscaped to appear eerie during the day, looked terrifying at night.

At last they came to the faerie mound and both girls stopped and stared. The only light was from the torch, one small drop in an ocean of darkness. In the rest of Blarney it was raining, but over the faerie mound snow was falling. The gently whirling flakes cascaded down and coated the small hill, moving in a different world from the hurrying rain.

'Now do you believe me?' said Maddy, her voice sounding too loud in the crushing dark. She touched the cross under her T-shirt with the tips of her fingers before dropping the rucksack on the ground and taking the knife from one of its front pockets.

'That can't be real; it has to be a trick,' said Roisin, her voice trembling with fear.

'Trust me, it's real,' said Maddy grimly. She crouched on the ground, the paring knife in one hand. 'C'mere, boy,' she whispered, winding the lead around her other hand as she dragged George closer.

'Don't!' hissed Roisin. 'Let's go back to Granny and Granda's and get someone to help. There must be an explanation for all this.'

'No one is going to help. This is the only way to get Stephen back,' said Maddy as she took the dog's collar off and held him by the scruff of the neck.

George could sense something coming that he wouldn't like and he cowered as she gripped him between her knees. She pinched the scruff of his neck between her thumb and forefinger and cut into the soft fatty flesh there. The dog yammered and twisted in her grip, but she held him tight until some of his blood had stained her hand and then she wiped it on the snow-covered mound, leaving a watery pink stain.

'Sorry, boy,' she whispered, as she dropped the knife

and hugged the shocked animal close. She plastered his smelly head with kisses and rummaged in the rucksack again. She found the biscuits and fed him one to cheer him up.

'That's it?' said Roisin.

'Of course,' said Maddy. 'You didn't think I was going to kill him, did you?'

Roisin sagged with relief and flopped down next to Maddy. 'Now what?'

'I don't know,' said Maddy glumly. 'This is about as far as my plan goes.'

They sat in the dark, waiting for something to happen. Maddy was oblivious to her cold, wet bum. She had no idea what to do next.

Then she heard sounds of thrashing leaves and snapping twigs as something made its way toward them through the bushes. The hair went up on George's back and he began to growl. Roisin sucked in a breath and grabbed Maddy's arm.

'It sounds big,' said Maddy, her mouth dry with fear. 'Did Google say what the guide would be?'

Roisin shook her head and her eyes filled with tears.

Something leaped out of the undergrowth at them. Maddy and Roisin screamed and scrambled backwards, before they heard the high, mocking laughter.

'Danny!' said Roisin. 'You scared me.'

'Shouldn't be out here then, should you,' he sneered. 'Mammy's good little girl is in a lot of trouble.'

'You haven't told Mam, have you?' Roisin's voice filled with terror.

'I didn't have to. Granny woke up and found you gone and she called Mam. Half the village is out looking for you, and Mam is going mental,' said Danny, delighted. 'The two of you are *so* dead. Granda isn't going to stick up for you this time, Maddy.'

'How long have you been following us?' she asked.

'Ages.' He grinned. 'I wanted to see if you were going to do us all a favour and take my fat sister with you when you ran away .' Roisin's face crumpled and she huddled into herself.

Maddy looked at Danny, who still had that evil grin on his face. 'You git,' she said quietly, and then she took a swing and her fist connected with Danny's nose. She felt the brief comfort hitting someone always brought, before Danny hit her back, then cannoned into her with all his weight. The breath went out of Maddy's body in a whoosh as her back jarred against the ground. She coughed and wheezed as Danny straddled her, aiming lazy punches at her face. She warded off a couple of blows before bringing her knee up hard into his back, breaking his concentration long enough for her to land a good left hook straight on the jelly of his eye. He yelled and clapped a hand to his face, while Roisin shouted at them to stop. Then Maddy bucked her hips hard and punched Danny in the chest, heaving him off her. As he crashed to the ground, she sprang up and sat on his chest, twisting the cotton of his sweatshirt in one fist while she raised the other to bring it down hard on his face. But before she could drop her knuckles she felt a large, strong hand clamp around her wrist.

'Here, here, enough of this!' a loud voice boomed as huge hands lifted her up into the air and shook her by the scruff of the neck. She glared at Danny around the torso of a giant of a man and had to be shaken a couple of times before she stopped trying to make a grab for him.

'Enough of this! What's going on here?' boomed the man. He bent to take a look at Maddy's face. 'I know you – you're Bat Kiely's granddaughter, aren't you?'

Maddy recognized Seamus Hegarty, a groundsman on the Blarney estate and a friend of Granda's. She was bound to get in trouble now.

'What are you doing in here at night? You know you're not supposed to be here.'

'Nothing,' said Maddy.

'She's trying to sacrifice the dog,' said Danny. 'It's a sick Halloween joke. She's trying to raise the Devil.'

'Shut up!' yelled Maddy, and went for him again,

lashing out with her feet as Seamus pulled her back. She kept kicking even when he shook her so hard her teeth hurt, and then she found herself being lifted off the ground and the collar of her jacket cut into her windpipe. She felt the blood rush to her face and she gasped and clawed at his hands, her legs kicking empty air. She heard Roisin scream.

'Putting blood on the mound, eh?' he growled. His eyes glowed up at her and she saw his pupils were round and silver like full moons. 'Little girls should be very careful what they wish for.' She thought she saw the shadow of antlers over his head, a full spread like a stag's, before everything went black.

And then it was very, very quiet.

chapter nine

Maddy opened her eyes to find herself lying flat on her back, the rucksack digging into her spine. The sky above her was a flat metallic grey, but there was no rain, no snow. The ground felt funny.

She sat up quickly in a flurry of what looked like black sand, and millions of particles rose to streak the air around her like smoke. They took an age to spin and fall back to the ground, their jet facets glittering and twinkling in the dim light. Overhead, a pale sun burned weakly through the grey haze and the black sand stretched as far as she could see. She got up slowly, sand bouncing and swirling in time with each movement of her legs and arms, clinging to the air around her. She trudged to where she could see Roisin and Danny lying on the ground. They groaned and began to sit up.

'Where are we?' said Danny.

'Where's George?' said Roisin. 'George? George? C'mere, boy!'

Maddy felt her heart sink. Then she looked around and spied a little splash of white against the black. She stumbled forward, feeling heavy-limbed and dazed, to where George sat staring listlessly into space. He looked up at her as she bent to pick him up and wagged his tail half-heartedly, curling into her stomach as she zipped him into her jacket. Roisin glared at Maddy as she flopped back down next to her, George's little face peeking out from under her chin.

'OK, so where are we then?' she demanded.

Maddy shrugged. 'I haven't a clue. You're supposed to be the expert.'

'Why? Because I looked some stuff up on the Internet?' said Roisin. 'Where are we? I want to go home.'

'If you didn't want to be here, then why did you follow me?' said Maddy.

'I didn't know you were doing . . . this. Besides, I didn't want you to get into trouble,' said Roisin.

'More like you couldn't bear to be left out of anything,' said Maddy. 'No way anyone could do anything around here without having you tag along, is there? Why don't you take a day off from yourself and—'

'WILL THE TWO OF YOU SHUT UP AND TELL

ME WHAT IS GOING ON?' roared Danny. 'Where the bloody hell are we?'

Maddy shot Roisin a look out of the corner of her eye. It was going to be very embarrassing explaining all this and she could see Roisin's cheeks turning pink already. She told Danny the whole story, bracing herself for his reaction.

'Faeries!' he spat. 'I know you're a dreamy eejit, Roisin, with your head always stuck in a book, but I thought you had a little bit more sense, Maddy. Why not say little green men had carried him off?'

'You're right, Danny, it's all in my head,' said Maddy, as she crossed her arms over a whimpering George. 'I'm making the whole thing up. That's why we're in the middle of a desert full of oddly behaved black sand. It's because I'm bonkers.'

Danny glared at her but he couldn't help it – his eyes slid away to look at the ground and he went quiet.

'Have you noticed there's no weather here?' said Roisin, as she lifted her hands from the sand and watched it swirl around her fingertips.

'What are you on about now?' said Danny impatiently.

'Think about it,' said Roisin, still staring at her hands. 'It looks like we're in a desert, but I don't feel hot or cold – or anything at all, to be honest.'

Maddy thought about this for a second and then licked her finger and held it up. 'No wind,' she said.

Danny sniffed. 'No smells either,' he said.

'This is a nothing place,' said Roisin.

Danny and Maddy looked at each other in panic.

'A nothing place? What's a nothing place?' said Danny. 'Are we in *purgatory*?'

'I dunno. Are faeries Catholics?' asked Roisin.

A cool breeze sprang up. The sand fought against it but was driven back through their hair and clothes.

'There's someone out there,' said Maddy, pointing straight ahead. They squinted into the distance and saw something white reflecting the rays of the weak sun.

It was moving toward them, its shape becoming clearer until Maddy could see it was a white stag with a massive spread of antlers and a heavy gold collar hung around his neck that winked in the light. The creature came to a stop in front of them, his velvety nose twitching in the scentless air.

The stag looked at Maddy and lowered his head until she was gazing directly into his wet brown eyes. She gulped as she realized that she couldn't see pupils – just twin images of a full moon in a dark sky filled with scudding clouds.

Ask me for help, said a voice in her head. She stared at the stag in shock.

'Did anyone else hear that?' said Danny, his voice shaking.

Ask me for help.

'Maddy, he's talking to *you*. Say something,' hissed Roisin.

'Like what?'

'Asking where we are would be a blinding start,' said Danny.

'Um, where are we?' she asked the stag, who still hadn't blinked.

You are on the border of what you know and what you believe.

'Are we in the faerie mound?'

Yes.

'This doesn't look like Tír na nÓg,' said Roisin. 'None of the books and faerie tales I read ever mentioned a desert.'

What you seek is within your reach. But until you believe in it, you cannot pass the border.

'Can we go back?' asked Danny.

Only if you know the way.

Maddy looked around them at the expanse of desert that stretched as far as the eye could see. There was nothing to break the monotony – no road, no landmark, not even a lump of sand-blasted, wind-scoured rock.

'Do you know the way?' asked Maddy.

The stag said nothing.

'Are you our guide?' asked Roisin.

The stag lifted his head up high and looked down his nose at them with his front feet neatly placed together.

What you already know is your guide and your map.

Maddy walked up to the stag, who inclined his head regally. 'So if we want to go forward into Tír na nÓg, we have to believe that we will walk into it, right?'

Yes.

'So all we have to do is wish it really hard and it will appear?'

You have to see it and believe it enough to step into it.

'Will this map also help us get home?'

The stag stood still as a statue as the soft breeze played around his hoofs.

'This is madness,' said Danny to the stag. 'No offence, but we can't just click our heels and say, "There's no place like home."'

'Well, we can't phone someone to come and pick us up either,' said Maddy .

'How do you know?' said Danny, his face lighting up with hope. He pulled his mobile from the back pocket of his jeans and checked the screen. His face fell. 'No signal.'

'Shocking,' said Maddy.

'Can we trust you?' asked Roisin in a small voice. The

stag swung his antlers to look at her. 'I don't mean to insult you, but I have no idea if you are a friend or an enemy, so how can I simply go where you tell me to go? How do I know I can get home by the path you want me to take?'

I did not think that going home was your purpose. Going home seems like a very poor sort of quest.

'Home is always the goal in stories, isn't it?' Maddy said. 'Heroes are always trying to go home or save home, so it seems good enough to me. If I do what you say, can I go home?'

The stag cocked his head at Maddy. *How do I feel to you? Fair or foul?*

Maddy stared up into the brown eyes. 'You feel fair,' she whispered.

'What are you saying, Maddy?' asked Roisin.

'I think he's asking us to trust our instincts,' she replied.

They all stood for a moment and looked at the stag, their breathing harsh and ragged in the silence. Power radiated from him like an electrical field and Maddy found herself struggling against the temptation to kneel.

'Will you come with us?' she asked.

This is a task I cannot help you with.

'Why not?'

Tonight, time is in chaos. My power ebbs. The stag

shook his head, his twin moons blotted by cloud. *But I offer you the way into the kingdom of the Tuatha de Dannan.*

'If you're not strong enough, what chance do we have?' said Maddy.

You are stronger than you think. There is magic in the old ways, in the human stories. What you know will bring you great power.

'I have no idea what that means,' said Maddy.

The moons came out from behind their clouds and the stag's eyes shone silver. *You will.*

Maddy looked at Roisin and Danny. They both shrugged.

'When I used to think about Tír na nÓg,' she softly, 'I imagined it as a place that shimmered, where you were never hungry or cold, and flowers bloomed everywhere and faeries flew about like birds. Is that what you mean?'

'I always thought it would be a place of everlasting twilight,' said Roisin, a blush stealing over her cheeks. 'White flowers scattered through the grass and tall trees. Faerie halls covered in jewels, filled with music and singing.'

See it.

Maddy closed her eyes and reached back into her mind for memories that had faded over time, of a world she had once tumbled into with every book, every Christmas special on TV.

'I think of dryads whose faces appear in the bark of trees and mermaids washing their hair in waterfalls,' said Roisin. 'Winged horses with golden bridles and faeries singing in the forest.'

'Dragons and animals that talk,' said Danny, blushing as Roisin stared at him.

Maddy grinned as the breeze whipped itself up into a stiff wind and in the distance the sand began to rise into the air. 'Unicorns and maidens, faeries curled up in flowers, stars that sing, magic castles in the clouds . . .'

'It's working!' yelled Roisin, as the wind rose to a howl, tearing at their clothes, and the stag threw back his head to bugle at the sky.

'Brownies and bogles, pixies and sprites, hollow hills bathed in candlelight!' yelled Maddy, excitement rising in all of them as the curtain of sand swept over them and the white stag disappeared from their sight.

chapter ten

Maddy had her eyes squeezed shut and the first thing she felt was cold air billowing around her, wrapping her in its sharp embrace. After the tasteless air of the nowhere place, the scent of wet pine and crushed grass tickled her nostrils. Roisin gasped, sending butterflies whirling through Maddy's stomach. Then she heard Danny say, 'It's beautiful!' and she opened her eyes.

It was.

They were standing on a grassy hilltop looking down on to dense forest. The sun hovered on the edge of the horizon, its dying rays sending prisms of light slicing through the crystal cold air to bathe them in shimmering colours. The forest canopy was covered in snow and in the distance before them a white tower twisted into the sky. Blue mountains smudged the horizon beyond the tower, while a vast river wound away from it, cutting through the forest as it rushed toward the far horizon on their left. Gradually the ranks of trees thinned out and a dry and barren land clung to the riverbanks. Lights twinkled among the trees and they could hear singing, as pure and sweet as the highest notes of a violin, held in an aching treble. Flocks of birds wheeled above the treetops looking to roost, their iridescent feathers flashing jewel bright in the sunset. A breeze lifted from the treetops and danced toward them, wrapping their faces in a wild perfume. Maddy closed her eyes and breathed deeply. She could smell crushed flowers, leaf mould, pine needles and bark, feather and fur. It was as if the forest had breathed out. She opened her eyes and looked down and for a second saw her feet clad not in trainers but tiny cloven hoofs. She blinked and the image was gone.

Roisin started to laugh and held an arm up to the dancing light. The fractured rays slid down her skin in blue-hued bracelets. 'We did it!' she cried. 'We are actually in Tír na nÓg.' George wriggled down from Maddy's arms and ran about in circles, barking.

Danny sat down hard on the snow-dappled grass. 'Is this happening?' he said, his expression stunned as he looked around.

'I don't know,' said Maddy, her eyes wide. 'It's unbelievable.'

'Oh, can't you feel it?' said Roisin gleefully. She giggled and spun on her heels, arms flung out.

'Feel what?' asked Maddy.

'The magic in the air. It's like licking a battery,' said Roisin. 'The whole place *hums* with it. I feel so good, so good, so *gooooood*!'

Roisin twirled and sang, her joy radiating out from her and lapping against Maddy like a wave. She began to giggle, and as she looked at Danny his normally scowling face broke into a smile. Seconds later they were all laughing on the hillside.

'Hang on,' Roisin said, stopping in her tracks and frowning at something behind them. 'Am I really seeing that?'

Maddy twisted her head to look behind her, and with a shock she recognized the faerie mound in the Blarney Castle. It topped the hill, dark and silent in the face of the sunset. Its shadows were unnatural, pooling around its feet and ringing it in darkness, rather than stretching away behind it..

'That's not the same mound, is it?' asked Danny.

'It can't be,' said Maddy.

'Maybe it is,' said Roisin. 'Maybe it exists in both places at the same time. You know, like parallel universes.'

'Is that possible?' asked Danny.

'At the moment, I'd believe in anything,' said Roisin.

Maddy studied the mound carefully. For a second it blurred. Then it shifted back into focus again with a sharp buzzing noise she could *feel* crawling around inside her head. She shuddered. 'It certainly looks like the one at the castle. I think we should head back here as soon as we've found Stephen.'

The laughter faded out of their eyes as they looked about them.

'Any ideas about how we do that?' asked Danny.

'Well, that tower is the only sign of civilization we have seen so far,' said Maddy, 'so I say we head for that and see if anyone there can help us. He might even be there.'

'You said this faerie stole him,' said Roisin. 'What are we going to do if he doesn't want to give him back?'

Maddy shifted the rucksack on her back and heard the pokers clank against the horseshoe. 'We'll have to deal with that when we find him.'

'It doesn't sound like much of a plan,' said Danny.

'It's not, but feel free to think of a better one,' said Maddy as she whistled for George. 'Right now, I suggest we get going.'

'We don't know how to get to that tower!' said Danny, as Maddy began to walk down the hill, Roisin skipping ahead, while George ran in giddy rings.

'Is it going to come to you sitting on wet grass in the middle of who knows where?' asked Maddy over her shoulder.

Danny shrugged and followed them down the hillside.

They plunged into the dense forest, the evergreen canopy blocking the sky. They were pleased to find there was a path and followed it. Now and then they heard the sound of sweet singing drifting to them through the air and saw lights bobbing among the trees. Sometimes tall, elegant creatures who radiated light passed close by carrying lanterns, the warm yellow glow bathing their lovely faces. As the faeries glided over the forest floor, turning to talk to one another, their laughter tinkling like bells and their richly embroidered clothes rustling and whispering, the children crouched in the undergrowth like rabbits, their hearts beating in their throats.

Maddy wanted to stare at their perfect faces, but for some reason the sight of the faeries made her mind blank with panic. They were beautiful, like paintings come to life, but their eyes and faces were hard and cold. She could see jewelled daggers sparkling at their waists and something told her there was a good chance she wouldn't wake up if she ever fell asleep in their company. Roisin and Danny were quiet and white-faced when they saw the faeries, so she knew they felt the same way.

Not all were lovely. As they hid from one shining group, a darker faerie hurried along in the bright ones' wake. This creature was stooped and wrapped in a murky cloak that covered even its feet. A chill radiated from it rather than light, and as it passed them Maddy caught a glimpse of a twisted, cold face.

The further into the woods they went, the fewer faeries there were. The forest was dark and thick here, a wilder place. Brightly coloured birds swooped and fluttered around them, perching on snow-crusted branches to sing silvery songs that bubbled from their throats. Soon the air was thick with songbirds and Maddy held her face and hands up as they swept over. The breeze from their wings puffed against her skin, bringing the scents of wild flowers and wet grass as they brushed their soft, feathered bodies against her chilled fingertips.

The gloom lightened as hundreds of tiny faeries appeared in a cloud and mingled with the birds, light pulsing from their bodies as their translucent wings beat as fast as a hummingbird's. These sprites swarmed, sparks streaking in their wake. They raced the songbirds and tickled their bellies, lifted strands of Maddy's and Roisin's long hair and tugged, and pinched and stroked any bare skin they could find. They whirled around Danny, spinning a web of candy-coloured sparks. He laughed and held out his hands to the little creatures, tempting them to sit on his palms. The faeries ignored him and whirled faster and faster, sparks fizzing and spraying into the air. The colours shivered across the snow and lit up his face like fireworks.

'This is *wonderful*!' he cried.

One faerie broke away and came to hover in front of Maddy. She stared at her for a moment before a smile split her tiny face. Then she leaned forward and touched the tip of Maddy's nose.

'Ouch!' Maddy yelled, as pink and blue sparks flew and a jolt of electricity ran through her.

The faerie giggled and circled her finger at Maddy.

'Buzzzzz,' she said.

'Don't you dare!' said Maddy. She lifted her hands up and clapped them hard. 'Or else!'

The faerie gave an indignant squeak, her face clouded with anger. She took off into the trees above, her friends racing to join her. Sparks rained down and the air filled with the smell of singed hair. Maddy brushed her hands over her head to feel blackened strands break and fall away from her fingers.

'Oh Maddy, why did you scare them off?' asked Roisin. 'They won't come back now.'

'I didn't fancy getting barbecued by your little friends, that's why,' said Maddy.

'Hey, one of them is coming back,' said Danny. 'C'mere, girl – I won't hurt you.'

The same little faerie who had tried to set light to Maddy's nose fluttered down in front of Danny.

'I'd watch her if I were you . . .' Maddy began, but it was too late. The faerie gripped one of Danny's fingers. Her body glowed white and then the light pulsed up Danny's arm.

'Ow, that really hurts!' he cried. The little faerie simply stuck her tongue out and flew up into the trees.

Maddy laughed. It was good to see Danny on the receiving end for once. She glanced down at the lead wrapped tightly around her fist and looked for George, whom she had forgotten in all the excitement. She really shouldn't have let him loose, but she was surprised to see him walking close behind her, his nose almost touching her heel.

She was relieved the grizzled old terrier had decided to behave himself – she didn't need him chasing off after animals in here; she had no idea if she would get him back.

A quick movement in the darkness beneath the trees caught her eye. It wasn't much, a flicker of a lighter shadow, but it was enough. Something else was walking with them. She peered harder into the trees and saw what the birds and faeries had stopped her from seeing before.

Long, dark shapes glided close to the ground, keeping pace with them as they walked along the path. Now and then, huge green eyes gleamed before the animal turned its head away and loped on. She could see them moving on either side of the path and realized they were surrounded.

George hadn't been behaving – he had caught the scent of wolves.

Maddy watched as the little terrier carefully avoided looking to the left or right. He stooped lower and lower until he was practically crawling on his belly. When Maddy picked him up and hugged him close he tucked his face into her armpit.

She wanted to warn Danny and Roisin, but she was terrified to make a noise or do anything to break the tension. It was obvious the wolves knew they were there, but Maddy kept her eyes ahead and hoped that if she ignored them, they would leave them alone.

Roisin was still giggling over the faeries while Danny walked ahead of them all in a huff, his pride injured. But after a while the silence pressing in around them became too obvious. Maddy saw Roisin look around, a frown on her face. When she spotted the wolves she drew in a breath to scream, but Maddy grabbed her arm from behind. Danny looked back at them.

'What's wrong now?' he said.

Just then a wolf stepped into a patch of light and looked straight at Danny, its tongue lolling from its mouth. Danny looked back at Maddy, his own mouth opening in a panicked O, but she hurried past him, dragging Roisin with her.

'Don't say anything, don't look at them, don't wind them up,' she whispered as she overtook him. 'Just keep walking'.

Now Maddy realized how quiet the forest was. There was no trill of songbirds, nor the click of magpies or the harsh cry of a crow. The only sound was their breathing and the occasional thump of snow sliding from an overladen branch. The wolves were silent and loped by the path, their huge paws stepping lightly over the carpet of leaf mould and pine needles.

Maddy desperately searched the gloom for help: for someone, for a shack with a door that could be locked – anything. But there was no other sign of life beneath the dripping trees. Only the dark, shaggy shapes that drifted like smoke, keeping time with their footsteps.

'Why are they not attacking us?' whispered Danny as his eyes darted from side to side.

'I don't know,' said Maddy. 'Maybe they want us to run.'

'Why?'

'They like playing with their food?'

'Are they herding us?' asked Roisin.

'They haven't made us go anywhere yet; they're just following,' said Danny.

'It's Little Red Riding Hood,' said Roisin.

'What are you on about?' said Danny.

'Little Red Riding Hood,' said Roisin. 'It's obvious. The wolf got her because she was a bad girl and left the path. We're staying on it so they can't attack us.'

'Rubbish,' said Danny.

'Have you got a better idea about what's going on?' asked Maddy.

'No, but I mean, they look like normal wolves,' said Danny. 'Unless someone read them the book, they don't know anything about Little Red Riding Hood. Which means, if they are hunting us, staying on the path isn't going to help. I'm climbing a tree. You should always climb trees if you think a wild animal is going to attack you.'

'No, don't!' squeaked Roisin. 'Step off the path and they'll get you. You have to stick to the rules. The stag said what we know would guide us.'

'You two can do what you like,' said Danny, 'but I'm not sticking around to become a main course.'

Before either Maddy or Roisin could stop him, Danny stepped off the path toward the nearest tree. Instantly a shaggy grey wolf burst from the undergrowth and with a snarl leaped at him. He went down in a tangle of limbs.

'Help, help!' he screamed. 'Get him off me!' He beat at the wolf's head as the animal bit into his arm and tried to drag him deeper into the undergrowth.

Roisin stood frozen but Maddy dropped George on the path and rushed to help Danny. She shrugged the rucksack from her shoulders as she ran and unzipped it, pulling out the poker. Running full tilt into the wolf, she smacked it hard across the ribs with the iron rod. The animal yelped and let go of Danny to turn to face her. It growled and bared its huge fangs, eyeing the poker as she held it before her like a sword. Its ears swivelled round as Danny scrambled to his feet and made a dash back to the path. Maddy kept her eyes locked on the wolf's as she stepped back slowly. The animal began to retreat itself, growls still rumbling in its throat, until the gloaming swallowed it whole.

'That thing nearly had the arm off me!' said Danny, his voice shaking.

'Are you surprised, you prat?' snapped Maddy. 'You should have listened to Roisin. They're not coming anywhere near us now.'

'We've got to stay on the path. Stay on the path and we're fine,' said Roisin, still rigid with shock. 'We follow the rules and we'll be OK. It's just a faerie tale, and nothing really bad ever happens in faerie tales.' She looked at Maddy. 'We can't get hurt in here, right?'

'Roisin, the big bad wolf *ate* Little Red Riding Hood, remember?' said Maddy. 'Did it hurt you much?' she asked Danny.

'I'm not too bad,' said Danny. 'My arm aches though.'

He got to his feet while Maddy scooped George up again. The little terrier was panting with fear and his breath rasped in the silence. She grabbed Roisin by the arm. 'Come on – let's keep moving.'

As soon as they started to walk, the loping shapes appeared again. Roisin flinched and let out a little sob. Maddy squeezed her arm. 'Just keep putting one foot in front of the other,' she whispered. 'This path has to lead somewhere.'

Then Maddy saw what was waiting for them up ahead. The forest opened out into a clearing filled with tall, frost-hardened grass. The path they were on led into the clearing, but there it stopped.

It was a dead end.

'What happens when the path runs out, Ro?' asked Danny.

'I don't know, do I?' snapped Roisin. 'It never runs out in the story.'

'Maybe this is what they want – a clear site, no trees to climb,' said Maddy.

'Then we won't go in,' said Roisin. 'Let's just turn around and walk back the way we came.'

'But that way doesn't get us home, Ro,' said Danny.

'I don't care,' hissed Roisin. 'I am *not* getting off this path.'

'I don't see that we have much choice, Danny,' said Maddy. 'Let's just turn around slowly and walk back. Sooner or later they'll give up and we can find another way to get to the tower.'

As the three of them turned to retrace their steps, a huge black wolf stepped on to the path in front of them. He planted massive paws in the grass to lower his head and snarl, showing what had to be the biggest pair of fangs Maddy had ever seen in her life. The hair on his back stood up as he paced toward them, narrowing his green eyes, his muzzle quivering as he peeled black lips back from his teeth. Saliva dripped from his mouth and his tail twitched behind him.

Carefully, all three children retreated, never taking their eyes off the wolf. His rasping snarl filled their ears and his paws moved forward slowly and deliberately. They found themselves backing into the centre of the clearing, where all around them wolf eyes glowed in the forest. The big black wolf stopped snarling, sat down in the centre of the path and curled his tail around his paws as neatly as a cat. He stared at them. The silence stretched tight.

'What do we do now?' whispered Maddy, as George trembled in her arms.

'I know it didn't work last time, but I think we should climb a tree,' said Danny.

'But that means running toward them,' said Roisin. 'We'll never make it.'

The black wolf threw his head back and let out a long, trailing howl that shivered the silence apart. The pack grew excited and Maddy could see them milling in the undergrowth, yipping and barking, but none joined in with the howl.

Suddenly he bounded toward them. They dropped to their knees and curled in on themselves, their arms wrapping around their heads, as he leaped over them and raced away into the trees. The pack crashed after him, all grace gone as they chased after their leader.

The children stayed where they were for a few seconds, not daring to move a muscle. Maddy's mind was numb with fear and she kept waiting to feel the wolf's hot breath on the nape of her neck. What she could feel was wet seeping through her jacket. She looked down at her clothes and the spreading yellow stain.

'I don't believe this!' she yelled as she held George away from her.

'What's wrong?' asked Roisin.

'It's George – he peed all over me!' said Maddy.

Roisin and Danny looked at each other and burst into hysterical laughter.

'It's not funny!' yelled Maddy, which made them laugh so hard they bent double, clutching their stomachs. She held George up in front of her face, his belly wet. 'You're a bad, bad dog,' she scolded. He wagged his tail sheepishly and licked her face in apology.

Danny and Roisin subsided into giggles, while Maddy ripped up handfuls of the frosty grass and tried to wipe her jacket clean. She nudged George with her knee. 'You could do with a wipe as well,' she said.

'What was that all about then? Why didn't that wolf go for us?' said Danny in a very shaky voice.

'I have no idea,' said Maddy. 'I am just glad he wasn't feeling peckish.' She staggered to her feet. Her legs were rubbery with shock. 'Well, the path stops here. I can't see a clear way through the trees,' she said. 'We are going to have to leave it if we want to keep going forward.'

'Nuts to that,' said Danny.

'Leave the path?!' yelled Roisin. Tears started to well up in her big brown eyes. 'You want us to do the one thing we know is going to get us eaten? Why do you think we should listen to you anyway? It's your fault we're here, your stupid idea to go after Stephen.' She started to cry.

Maddy looked at Danny, who shrugged his shoulders in disgust.

'I'm not standing around here waiting for them to come back,' he said. 'She's blubbing so much we wouldn't hear them sneaking up on us. I'm going to climb a tree and see if I can spot a way out of here.'

He went over to a huge old pine tree and started looking for a way up.

'I did tell you to stay home, Roisin. I never asked you to come after me,' Maddy said.

'Wherever you go, there's trouble,' Roisin sobbed.

Maddy felt hurt. She opened her mouth to say something back, but Roisin sighed and wiped at her eyes with the back of her hand. 'Sorry,' she sniffed. 'I'm a bit freaked out.'

'Um . . . yeah . . . no, that's understandable,' said Maddy, surprised.

'I *hate* it when I cry,' said Roisin, scrubbing at her wet face. 'It doesn't mean I'm a coward, you know. I just cry easily, that's all.'

'I never said you were,' said Maddy.

'*He* does,' said Roisin fiercely, jabbing her chin in Danny's direction. 'He thinks I'm a crybaby.'

'I'm not Danny,' said Maddy quietly. Roisin looked at her for a moment and then offered a watery smile.

Embarrassed, Maddy looked toward Danny to see how he was doing, but he was standing as if rooted to the spot. She frowned and walked over to him.

'What's up with you?' she asked.

'The tree is staring at me,' said Danny, his eyes never leaving the trunk of the pine.

'Come again?'

'The. Tree. Is. Staring. At. Me,' said Danny in a low voice. 'And it doesn't look happy.'

CHAPTER ELEVEN

Maddy glanced at the tree and saw two brown eyes that glared at her malevolently. They flicked between her and Danny, then began to roll menacingly as the two of them took a step back. Suddenly, the eyes shot forward and a woody mouth splintered apart.

'BOO!' it shouted.

Maddy and Danny stumbled backwards and watched, open-mouthed, as a piece of bark began to pull itself away from the tree and clamber down to the ground. As it walked toward them with a rolling gait, she could see a short body with long arms and legs, finished off by huge hands and feet that sported long, knobbly fingers and toes. What she at first thought was a branch with a couple of leaves perched gamely on the end of it turned out to be the creature's nose. Its head stopped at about mid-thigh on Danny and it cocked its head to look up at them. Its massive eyes blinked in its woody face.

'What is it?' whispered Danny.

'It's a dryad,' breathed Roisin behind them. 'A faerie that lives in trees.'

'I's not an *it*!' the woody man snapped.

'Sorry,' said Roisin, turning crimson. 'I didn't mean to offend. It's just that . . .'

'Doesn't matter if you didn't mean to; you did,' he said.

They looked at each other. Maddy cleared her throat. 'Well, my name is Maddy and this is Danny and Roisin.'

'Pleased to meet you,' Danny and Roisin murmured.

They all stood there, shifting uneasily from foot to foot as the little man continued to glare at them.

Maddy decided to try again. 'What's your name?'

'None of your business.'

'But we told you our names!' protested Maddy.

'Don't care. Didn't hear me ask for them, did you?' said the dryad.

'Oh for pity's sake, Hobbs, tell them your name and try to be a little bit civil,' sighed a voice above them. Another piece of pine tree began to climb down toward them. This one was taller and thinner than Hobbs and stiff pine needles sprang out from his head like an Afro.

'Civil? To this lot?' shrieked Hobbs. 'You know what they are, don't you, Izzie? Men! Great big stinking sacks of meat – you can smells them for miles! And with men come fire and axes.'

'We don't mean any harm!' cried Roisin. 'And we haven't got any axes or matches or anything like that.'

'But you've got iron,' said Hobbs. 'I can smells it; the whole forest tastes of it.'

The forest began to rustle and the trees that surrounded the clearing shivered as more dryads climbed down. They began to gather around, creaking and rustling, one or two of them smacking their own jaws to get them working.

The clearing filled with dryads. Soon the air was busy with their chattering. Even the enormous trees seemed to bend down as if to listen. They waved their hands as they talked, and Maddy noticed some of them jabbing their fingers in her direction. A slim dryad female with silver hair and skin and black eyes was making her way to the front of the crowd.

Roisin took a step toward Izzie and Hobbs, who were arguing fiercely in a scratchy language. She cleared her throat. 'Excuse me,' she said. 'I don't mean to interrupt, but could someone tell me where we are?'

Hobbs snorted. 'If you don't know that, girl, then you don't have much of an imagination.'

Izzie smiled at her. 'You're in an older world, a world that humankind barely remembers.'

'But we made this up,' said Danny.

At this there were angry murmurs in the crowd.

'How did you make this world up, human child?' asked Izzie.

'From stories and faerie tales – stuff we remembered from when we were little,' said Danny.

The dryads began to laugh.

'And where do you think these stories came from?' snorted Hobbs. 'They is echoes of what your ancestors remembered from when we walked the land with them, when they were squatting in their own filth and drawing on cave walls!'

'But I don't understand,' said Maddy. 'The stag told us what we knew would bring us power – we thought he meant magic, to help us get Stephen and go back home.'

The dryads began to talk very animatedly among themselves. Izzie grabbed Maddy by the arms. 'A stag let you in here, do you say? A white stag?'

'Yes, yes – do you know who he is? What did he mean when he said we would have power?'

Izzie looked at her with eyes full of pity. 'I think he meant that what you knew would guide you and help you stay alive,' he said.

Maddy stared back at him in horror. This was getting much too serious. She hadn't signed up for mortal danger.

Roisin stared at her with wide eyes. 'We're going to die?' she asked.

'Let's hope so,' said Hobbs.

Furious, Maddy turned on him. 'I've got a poker in my hand, you know. Do you want a smack?'

'Try it, meat-bag,' sneered the dryad.

'Stop it!' insisted Izzie, while Hobbs bristled indignantly. 'Go home, human child,' he advised sadly. 'There's no place for you in the woods and rivers wild. Your friend is lost.'

'He can't be,' said Maddy.

Izzie shook his head. 'The Winter Queen has him. There is no hope. Go home.'

'Who is the Winter Queen?' asked Roisin.

'Liadan – the wife of Cernunnos, the Horned God, and Queen of the Winter Court,' piped up a nut-brown dryad with a deeply wrinkled face.

Hobbs spat on the ground. 'Queen, if you please!' he sneered. 'She's an uppity elf and no better than she should be. If Cernunnos wasn't so taken with her big eyes he would have sent her and her family packing long ago.'

'Hush, Hobbs, you'll get in terrible trouble saying things like that,' said Izzie, his eyes scanning the forest around them, while the other dryads whimpered and cowered.

'Don't you shush me, I won't stands for it!' The little dryad was practically jumping up and down on the spot with rage. 'I am saying what all of you is thinking and none of you has the guts to say out loud. Cernunnos is befuddled and bewitched by a common elf. Nothing but trouble here since she and her kind arrived, dragging all kinds of human trash through the land. It's bad enough she takes them for pets, now we have to put up with their kith and kin chasing after them, stinking the place up with their iron.' He pointed a finger at Maddy. 'She lets a bunch of you in every now and then, and until you die in here we have to put up with the pollution of the worst of your emotions, the dregs of your id, every nightmare that haunts you. Go back to where you came from, you filthy, filthy creatures!'

With that, Hobbs turned and stomped up to his tree, melting away into the bark. Izzie wrung his hands and shifted nervously from foot to foot, swivelling his ears toward the rustling behind him as one by one the other dryads began to slip away from the clearing.

Maddy looked at him. 'This Liadan has taken kids before?'

He nodded. 'Every now and then since she came, we have seen her riding through the woods with a child asleep in her arms.'

'Has she ever given them back?'

'No one has ever come after them before,' said Izzie. 'And she already knows you are here. The wolves of the White Tower have been playing games with you – I saw.'

'The wolves are hers?' asked Danny.

'They are not faerie kind, but she gives them protection and they watch for her,' said Izzie.

'Help us!' said Roisin, rushing up to him. 'We can't leave him here; you must understand that. We'll go home as soon as we get him, and we can leave quicker with your help.'

The dryad's Afro quivered and his shoulders shook as he wrung his hands. 'No,' he said, his voice hoarse with fear. 'I can't do that. None of us can.'

Roisin's face crumpled with disappointment, but Danny looked over at Maddy, his expression hard and determined.

Maddy looked back at Izzie and swung the poker on to her shoulder.

'You're not going to help us?' she asked.

He shook his head.

'Well, get lost then. We're not a freak show.'

High, mocking laughter rang through the clearing, and the sharp sound of a slow handclap. The remaining dryads looked up and froze where they were, terrified.

What now? Maddy thought.

CHAPTER TWELVE

'Well said, little mortal,' said a harsh voice from a treetop. 'You would make a fine pet.'

'I'm no pet,' Maddy called out, searching for the speaker in the trees.

Snow thudded to the ground as a faerie sprang from a branch and fluttered gracefully down to land just in front of Maddy. Roisin gave a little scream and ran back through the clearing to cling to Danny. As Maddy's jaw dropped, she heard Danny suck his breath in behind her.

The faerie standing in front of her was no delicate little sprite. She loomed over Maddy, long and lean with ropes of muscle throughout her every limb. Maddy had to tip her head back to look at her; she was a good seven feet tall. Her skin was bone white and tattooed with pale grey Celtic patterns. Every inch of her was covered with the swirling marks, from the tips of her fingers to the edge of her hairline. Silver scars marked her, from fights she had probably won. Her long white hair was stiffened and combed high above her head and away from her face, dropping down her back. Everything about her, from her fingers to her face, was unnaturally long. Her nose was hooked and her mouth was thin and cruel. Her gossamer wings were covered in frost patterns, their beauty marred by a torn and trailing piece of skin and tissue in the lower half of the left wing. Her feet and legs were bandaged in soft white leather, and gold arm-rings bound straining muscles. Fine linen was wrapped around her breasts and between her legs, the skirt torn to the thigh and trailing behind her in ragged strips. A whip was coiled at her waist. Her eyes were blood red, with no whites and as cold and indifferent as a bird of prey's. She was terrifying and magnificent at the same time. The dryads huddled behind her looked like old sticks in comparison.

'Not all has been well today in this little paradise of ours,' said the faerie. She kept her eyes on Maddy as she paced around her. 'The stink of iron is in my nose and the rank taste of it on my tongue. The sun is taking an age to go down. It sits there, half over the horizon, and I can't get my beauty sleep. It puzzles me greatly. But then I smell blood and I rejoice, because it must be the Samhain Fesh, and mortals have come looking for war.' She stopped pacing and looked down at Maddy, her lip curling into a sneer. 'But what do I find? Insects, and no worthy opponent in sight.'

'The sun won't set?' Maddy heard Danny say behind her. His voice was high with relief. She looked over her shoulder at him. *What are you doing?* she mouthed. But he was so happy he just kept talking. 'Don't you see? He's helping us – the stag Cernunnos. You said we had to cross over on Halloween night – he's keeping the door open for us until we find Stephen.' He looked at the red-eyed faerie. 'Your boss is looking out for us, which means you can't touch us.'

Roisin hid her face in Danny's shoulder as the faerie paced closer. 'Is that so, little man?' she said, bending at the waist until her blood-filled eyes were level with Danny's. 'It's a pity for you that Cernunnos isn't my "boss". The stag doesn't scare the hound.'

'But . . . but he rules in here, right? He's the Horned God, the big cheese?' Danny gulped.

The faerie raised a pale eyebrow. 'Cernunnos does not hold sway in the Winter Court. My pledge is given to the Winter Queen, and no one else can command me.'

'Who are you, then, and what do you want?' asked Maddy.

The creature swivelled slowly on her heel and began to pace around Maddy again. 'I am Fachtna. I whip the hounds to the hunt, and when my queen calls for it I head her war band. I am the strong arm that strikes when my queen is displeased.' She bent down so fast Maddy had to take a step back. Her breath steamed in the air between them. 'You will show me respect.'

Maddy nodded.

Fachtna walked over to a huge oak and leaned against the tree. It shuddered and lifted its branches higher as her tattooed skin touched the bark. She looked at the dryads, who waited fearfully.

'Go,' she commanded. 'I have no business with dryads.'

Izzie gave Maddy an apologetic look, but he ran as fast as the others from the clearing. The little dryads melted away into their trees, and all that was left of them were a few leaves shaken loose from the branches that drifted in the wind.

Fachtna stretched out one scarred arm and examined her talons. 'You are fortunate, human child. My queen is wise and just. You amuse her. I've come here with a bargain.'

'I don't trust any faerie enough to bargain with them,' said Maddy.

Fachtna threw her head back and laughed, showing off teeth that had been filed to points.

'And you would be wise, little pet, not to do so,' she said. 'But I think you will like this contract.'

'I'm listening,' said Maddy.

'Queen Liadan finds your devotion to the mortal child touching. She bids me tell you that you may come to her in the White Tower and take him back. He is unharmed and she will not lay a finger on you until he is in your arms,' said Fachtna.

'And what do I have to give in return?' asked Maddy.

'You must provide her with sport,' said Fachtna. 'Once you have the child, you can try to go home. But the hunt will pursue you. I will chase you with my scucca hounds. And if I catch you, your life and that of your companions is forfeit.'

'What if we decide to turn around and go home now?' asked Danny.

Fachtna smiled at him. 'Then there is no contract and the hunt is unleashed. The deal is that you *all* come and you *all* run before me.'

'What's the catch?' Maddy asked. 'There always is a catch with you lot.'

'That's a puzzle for you to solve,' said Fachtna.

'Liadan . . .' began Roisin, before Fachtna stopped her with a glare. 'Sorry, *Queen* Liadan says she won't try to stop us coming for Stephen. Can any other faerie try to stop us or hurt us in any way?'

Fachtna smiled broadly. 'Clever pet – I'll let you die first. No, the promise is that no faerie may seek to do you harm. But you have to come on your own, with no help.'

'Can we have help getting away?' asked Maddy.

'If you can find any brave enough to give it,' said Fachtna.

Roisin and Danny looked at Maddy. 'I don't see what choice we've got,' said Roisin.

'Why should we agree to anything she says?' Danny objected. 'She could be telling us anything. It could be a trap.'

'Because faeries can't lie, can you?' said Roisin.

Fachtna put her hand on her heart and bowed low. 'My mouth is pure.'

'What's stopping you from just killing Stephen anyway?' asked Maddy.

'If we did that, you would not fight so hard or run so fast. You wouldn't have any hope to be crushed,' said Fachtna. 'Failed hope gives despair a much stronger taste.'

Maddy thought the terms of the contract over in her mind. She couldn't find a catch, but Granda had told her never to strike a bargain with a faerie. But then, Granda had never been this far from home.

'Fine,' she said. 'We come to you unopposed by any faerie, and we take Stephen back unharmed. Then we'll see what happens.'

'You give your word?' asked Fachtna.

'I give you my word,' said Maddy.

'*All* of you?' the faerie pressed.

Danny and Roisin looked at each other, their faces grim.

'We do,' they said.

'Your word is cast, as is my queen's,' said Fachtna. 'None can be released from it until you are dead or the hounds thwarted.' She smiled her ghastly smile. 'And I always catch my prey.'

With that she launched herself into the air, a white blur against the sky, and was gone.

Maddy sighed and her shoulders sagged under the weight of her fear. She had no idea what they had all just agreed to. She thought of her warm bed. *I want to sleep forever*, she thought. *I want to curl up under my duvet with a book and I want this all to go away when the book closes.*

Instead, she lifted George from Roisin's arms and put him on the ground, snapping the lead on to his collar. She pushed her way through the undergrowth and found the path continued ahead, starting up from the ring of trees as if the huge plants had simply shifted their weight on to it for a little while. She didn't look to see if Roisin and Danny were following, but she could hear them walking behind her.

No birds or little faeries came near them, and the forest was hushed. Every twig broken underfoot cracked through the silence and made them jump. As her fear subsided, Maddy began to get angry. She was cold, hungry and worn out with fear. She wanted someone to take out her temper on, and the more she thought about it, the more obvious it seemed.

She stopped on the path and turned to look at Danny.

He halted in front of her.

'What's up?' he asked.

'You know, for as long as I've known you, you've been a nasty, mouthy git who has no problem using his fists on people,' she said, as she got right up into his face. 'So do you want to explain what happened back there?'

'What do you mean?' he asked.

'Oh, you know, the wolves, the dryads, Fachtna issuing death threats, and you just standing there with your gob hanging open, letting me and Roisin do all the talking. It's just that you always seem so brave when you're picking on me or your sister, I was wondering why you turned so chicken when we really needed you to do something.'

Roisin groaned and threw herself down on the grass. 'Do you two have to get into it every half-hour? We're not going to get anywhere at this rate.'

'And where is it exactly that we're going, thanks to her?' said Danny. 'Did you hear her? She actually agreed to us being hunted. It's like a bad horror movie. I didn't sign up for this.'

'We all agreed to it, Danny,' said Roisin. 'We can't just keep wandering around in here – we had to do something'.

George lay down, put his head on his paws and sighed.

'Anyway, *you* didn't sign up for anything,' said Maddy. 'You're here because you just had to follow us and make fun of us. It serves you right.'

Danny stepped closer to her and glared at her, nose to nose. 'At least I've been watching what's been going on around us since we started walking again,' he hissed through clenched teeth.

Maddy narrowed her eyes at him. 'What's that supposed to mean?'

'This.' Suddenly Danny bounded to one side and dashed into the undergrowth after a fleeing white shadow that was running away from the path from tree to tree. There was scuffling and Danny came back, struggling with a creature that kicked and clawed. Panting, he threw it down at Maddy's feet. 'That little sneak has been following us for ages,' he panted.

'What are you doing?' Maddy challenged him, as she bent to help the creature up. 'You picked on a girl half your size!'

A pale dryad got slowly to her feet, her whole body trembling. Standing straight, she was still a head smaller than Maddy and very slight. Her eyes were jet black in her heart-shaped face, and long, thick silver hair reached to her heels. Her silver skin was covered in fine traces of emerald-green moss, and her lips and nose were smooth and polished. The hands that reached up to brush the dirt from her hair were long and delicate, as were her feet. She was very beautiful and very, very naked. Maddy hoped her thick hair didn't move too easily.

Roisin rushed over to her. 'I am *so* sorry. Are you hurt?'

The dryad gave her a sleepy smile. 'No.' George was sniffing at her, and Maddy pushed him away with her foot in case he decided she was more tree than girl and cocked his leg.

'What are you apologizing for, dimwit?' said Danny. 'She was following us – she could be Liadan, for all you know.'

The dryad broke into tinkling laughter while the girls rolled their eyes. 'Didn't you listen to what they were saying back there?' said Roisin. 'Liadan is an elf, and this girl is obviously a dryad . . . dimwit.'

'That still doesn't explain why she was following us, and you had better find out before you decide to be bestest friends,' said Danny. 'She could be working for Fachtna.'

'Fachtna no friend of mine,' said the dryad, wrinkling her little nose. 'But I help you till the trees are no more, bring you to the White Tower. And you make Winter go away.'

CHAPTER THIRTEEN

Before she would answer any questions, the dryad insisted they leave the path. 'Stay hidden,' she urged, holding a finger to her lips. 'Like little, little mice in the forest. No one must see.'

She led them to a hollow beneath the roots of an ancient oak. 'But first, I need heat. Snow everywhere; my tree is tired,' she said. 'I get too cold, I fall asleep, and you will be all alone.'

Maddy and Roisin curled around the dryad, who sighed and snuffled with pleasure as their body heat warmed her, sending a faint green blush through her skin. Danny refused to snuggle down with them and squatted between the iron-hard roots that arched above his head. 'No offence, but I don't want any body contact with my sister and my cousin. That's just too gross.'

'Sorry Danny got a bit rough with you, but why are you helping us?' Maddy said to the dryad.

The silvery faerie hid her face in her hair. 'It means talking about bad things,' she said. 'Bad, bad things. I doesn't like it.'

'I'm sorry, but we don't know what's happening here – you have to tell us,' said Maddy.

The creature sighed and her breath sounded like leaves rustling in the wind. She was so still and quiet Maddy wondered if she had gone to sleep. She was about to lift the thick locks of hair that covered the dryad's face to see if she was awake when the faerie started speaking in a small voice.

'Cernunnos and the Morrighan were the first of the Tuatha de Dannan to come to Ireland,' she began. 'He took the forests and the mountains to rule; she took the skies and the water. Their tribe followed them, and the Tuatha lived in your world when it was young, and mortals and faerie people worshipped them. They were so powerful, so strong. They could make the rain fall, the sun shine, the winds howl. But the Tuatha do not have many children, while men do. The tribes of men grew bigger and bigger, and when the Cross came and other men told them it was wrong to worship the Tuatha they turned against them and drove the Tuatha into the mounds and under the earth. They were gods no more to mortals. The Tuatha wept to be shut away from the mortal world, so the Morrighan slept and created a world of dreams for them, safe from the touch of mortals, where they would be forever young.' The dryad sobbed and fell silent.

'Tír na nÓg,' breathed Roisin. 'It means "Land of Eternal Youth".'

Maddy waited a little while as the dryad shook with misery. 'What happened then?' she prompted.

The little dryad sniffed and smiled sadly. 'Without humans to rule, the Tuatha fought. Each thought *they* should rule. The other faerie peoples tried to live on in your world, hidden from mortal sight, but with the coming of the Cross, the brownies, the trolls, the glaistigs and all their kind fled to the Land of Eternal Youth and pledged allegiance again to the Tuatha de Dannan. Cernunnos and the Morrighan wanted peace so they made eight of their tribe the Kings and Queens of Summer, Autumn, Spring and Winter and gave them equal power.'

'Why do it by seasons?' asked Danny.

'Because every season must come and go, so every court gets a turn at ruling and none can be stronger than the other,' said Roisin. 'Checkmate.'

'Did it work?' asked Maddy.

The little dryad shook her head. 'No. They fought and fought but could not win out against each other. But something happened to the Winter monarchs, and the Summer Court gained the upper hand,' she said. 'The Land was parched, and the forest burned. Chaos reigned, and the Morrighan struggled to bring the courts to peace.'

The trees around them shuddered and snatched their branches a little higher, as if they could still remember the pain of the flames licking at their trunks.

'How does Liadan fit in? Is she a Tuatha de Dannan?' asked Maddy.

The dryad shook her head. 'She is an elf, one of the faerie people from the cold northern countries. Liadan came to these shores with her kin on dragon-headed ships. They hunted and slashed and burned until the forest was nearly gone. The Morrighan and Cernunnos thought the elves were the answer. Liadan and her kind are strong – strong enough to take on the mantle of a Tuatha, or so the Morrighan thought. She offered the Winter Queen's crown to Liadan, so that Winter would once again balance the power of the Summer Court, and Cernunnos offered himself as a husband, to bind Liadan to the forest and stop her hurting us. With a non-Tuatha reigning over Winter, the courts could not join against the Morrighan and bend her to their will. Liadan agreed. She was greedy for a crown, but she didn't know what it would do to her.'

'What did it do?' asked Roisin.

'The crowns were forged with all the power of the season they rule. When Liadan took the Winter Queen's crown, she had to take Winter's cold as well,' said the dryad. She shook her head in despair. 'Liadan is an old and powerful elf, but the Winter crown was meant to be worn by a Tuatha. The Morrighan was wrong – Liadan did not have the strength to bear Winter. The crown's cold burns through her veins, twists her body, makes every step she takes, every tear of ice she cries, agony. The Morrighan's gift has made Liadan's mind as bent as her body. She has gathered dark faeries around her, and now the Winter Court is a bad place. With the Tuatha Winter Queen gone, her brethren have fled to other courts. No Tuatha will pay allegiance to Winter now; none of them will bend the knee to a crippled, foreign queen.'

'Why don't the other courts get rid of her, if she's so bad?' asked Danny.

The dryad smiled. 'The Tuatha hoard their power and they cannot bear to give it away, even to their own people. But someone must rule Winter. It's easier to let Liadan wear the crown for now than for the Tuatha to agree on who should take it from her.'

'Hobbs said she has had humans in her court,' said Maddy.

'Captives, all children,' said the dryad.

Maddy felt her throat close up with fear. 'What does she do with them?'

'I don't know.'

Maddy looked up at the forest canopy and blinked away the tears that gathered at the corners of her eyes. So this was the faerie who had Stephen. *He'll be so scared*, she thought.

'What does this have to do with Stephen?' asked Roisin.

'Since she took the little one, Liadan has been stronger,' said the dryad. 'Winter has come early and the cold bites and gnaws us. The balance is gone, and the other courts will go to war to bring it back – or to gain power themselves. The old trees say it was like this last time the Tuatha fought – the hush before the storm. Everyone is scared; everyone is hiding.'

The dryad sat up and curled her tiny hands into fists, her little face flushing a deeper green with anger. 'When the Tuatha de Dannan go to war, us all suffer. Us dryads are our tree's spirit made flesh,' she said. 'My tree is sick. Winter has been too long. Liadan will make the other courts angry if she does not give way, and who knows what war will bring? I don't want to die.' She looked at Maddy. 'The child makes Liadan strong. You take him, Winter goes away, war goes away.'

'How can he do that?' asked Maddy. 'He's still a baby.'

'Don't know,' said the dryad, shaking her head. 'But it must be him – we felt the change when he came.'

'Are we not forgetting one small but very important detail here?' said Danny. 'The deal is we get to the tower without any help. If you help us, the contract is broken.'

'Won't get there without me,' insisted the dryad.

'But the contract says that no faerie can harm or help us,' said Roisin.

'No *faerie*, no,' chuckled the dryad. 'But there is more than faeries in the forest. There are lots of ways for the unwary to come to harm and not by a faerie's hand.'

So there's the catch, Maddy thought.

'Fachtna said she would come after us with her scucca hounds,' said Danny. 'What does that mean?'

'"Scucca" means "demon" in the old tongue,' said the dryad. She went pale again and looked at Maddy. 'You made a bad, bad bargain. The scucca don't stop, don't rest. The fir dorocha, the dark men, faeries that breed fear and hatred, drive them on, and terror travels before them.'

Maddy looked at Danny and Roisin and could see the fear in their eyes.

'Fachtna called this place a paradise,' said Roisin sadly. 'It doesn't sound much like paradise to me.'

'It can be,' said the dryad softly.

'What's your name?' said Maddy.

The dryad smiled. 'Fionnghuala. It means "White Shoulders". Call me Fionn.'

It was hard keeping up with Fionn. She wanted them to get to the tower as fast as possible and they all stumbled after her as she glided from tree to tree as quick as a bird. As Maddy tripped over roots and twisted her ankle on rocks she looked longingly at the smooth path to her left. But shortly after they started they had to take cover as seven elves went running by. Fionn curled up into a tight little ball until they were gone and had to be coaxed into unbending long after they had disappeared from sight. It took even longer for the little dryad to stop shaking with fear.

Maddy felt as if they had been walking for hours. Her watch had stopped working, her feet were numb in her trainers and she had to suck her fingers to warm them up. Every now and then they stopped and huddled close to Fionn to warm her and keep her moving when she became sluggish and sleepy. Danny was horrified at being asked to press close to a naked female, but he compromised by standing back to back with Fionn, while Maddy and Roisin opened their jackets and held her close. Fionn refused to let them try and light a fire with Danny's lighter – the forest would be angry, she warned, even if they only burned dead wood and leaf litter.

Maddy fervently wished she had brought something more substantial than jam sandwiches. She had shared them with Danny and Roisin and now all they had left was biscuits.

Now and then, Fionn would ask them to wait while she went on ahead. They heard the great trees groaning and saw them thrashing their branches, before all was still and the dryad came back to lead them on again.

'Why do the trees behave like that?' asked Roisin as they stopped for what must have been the sixth time to watch the old trees groan and bend their creaking trunks slowly as Fionn talked to them.

'When tree and dryad become very old, they grows into each other,' said Fionn. 'The ancient trees in this forest can see and hear you. The young trees need their dryad to do that. But you can't talk to the old ones – they would lead you in circles until you died of hunger and thirst. The old ones don't like you, but they listens to me.'

They looked nervously at the trees around them and shuffled closer to Fionn.

'I don't understand why dryads get such a hard time here,' said Danny. 'You all seem pretty scary to me.'

Fionn scowled. 'Because we're not borned from faeries – we grow with our elements, and have no magic – other faeries thinks they are better than us. And the Tuatha de Dannan don't even notice us.'

Maddy looked at the brooding forest that surrounded them. *That could be a mistake*, she thought.

But it wasn't all fear and danger. As they scrambled down a rocky incline and steeled themselves to splash through an icy stream tumbling over slippery rocks, Fionn hustled them behind a tree and told them to hush.

'Not a word!' she hissed. 'Remember, like little mice.'

Maddy scooped George up and felt her stomach clench in dread as she wondered if the wolves had finally caught up with them. She was squeezed between Roisin and Danny and she could feel the same tension in them. Then she heard, or rather felt, a sound that throbbed through her whole body. Noise like whale music drifted upstream and the birds in the forest hushed. Even the trees leaned forward to catch the notes, and suddenly there appeared two unicorns, cantering through the stream, water spraying up from their legs and bursting into iridescent light as it caught the sun. The mare paused to drink and the stallion stood over her, gazing into the forest. She lifted her dripping muzzle and lipped at his neck, while he tossed his head and entwined his neck with hers, caressing her and calling out his throbbing song. The air around them shimmered and the outline of their white bodies burned blue. Rearing up, the mare bounded away and the stallion chased after her until they were lost from sight.

The forest kept its hush for a moment after the pair were gone, the haunting melody of their cries trailing off into the distance. Then the birds burst into song, their breasts swelling as they fought to sing louder, more joyously than their neighbours. Maddy found her cheeks were wet with tears. George wriggled happily in her arms and licked the tears away.

'Unicorns,' breathed Roisin, her eyes shining feverishly. 'They do exist!'

Fionn was grinning from ear to ear and looked more awake then they had seen her yet. 'They are old magic, created from the bones of the earth,' she said.

'We tell stories about them at home, but I never thought they existed,' said Roisin.

'You chooses not to believe in them and so you don't see them,' said Fionn, shrugging.

'It's that simple?' said Danny.

Fionn looked back at him and grinned. 'Yes, that simple.'

'How do we see them now?' asked Maddy.

'You believe in faeries now?' said Fionn.

'Good point,' said Maddy.

Just at that moment Danny's feet slipped on the

moss-covered roots of a massive oak and he tumbled face first into a puddle, covering himself in mud and black-brown leaf mulch. They all stared at him as he blinked in surprise, and before Maddy knew it, she and Roisin were bent double with laughter. George tried to lick Danny's face clean, his tail wagging at a million miles an hour, while Fionn rushed to help him up.

Furious, Danny pushed her helping hand away. 'Why the hell are we doing this anyway?' he snarled.

'What?' said Roisin.

'Why is it up to us to run to Stephen's rescue?' he demanded.

'You're not suggesting we just leave him?' snapped Maddy, her cheeks flushing red with anger.

'No, what I'm saying is, there are plenty of other people better able to rescue him than us. Like Cernunnos and the Morrighan. Where the hell are they?' He made a show of thinking for a second. 'Oh, wait, we know where Cernunnos is – he's in Blarney, on holiday.'

'What are you on about?' asked Maddy.

'Think about it. Seamus Hegarty happens to amble along just after you put blood on the mound, and before we all blacked out I could have sworn he was wearing a massive pair of antlers. Then a stag lets us in here – anyone else joining the dots?'

'Seamus Hegarty is Cernunnos?!' said Roisin. 'If

that's true, why is he in our world, and why has he sent us to do his dirty work?'

'In our world he is a white stag in the Winter, returning to animal form so he can be closer to the old magic while it sleeps with the earth. It is an ancient rite, but it makes him less powerful,' said Fionn. 'The longer Winter lasts, the stronger Liadan grows and the weaker Cernunnos becomes. I don't know why he is in your world too.'

'Well, I say we head back to Blarney and get Seamus, Cernunnos, whatever it is he calls himself, to sort this out,' said Danny.

'But I just told you, in our world he is a stag for the Winter,' said Fionn. 'He can't help us.'

'Fine,' said Danny through gritted teeth. 'Then we go to Plan B and get the Morrighan to help.'

'The Morrighan sleeps in the arms of the earth,' said Fionn. 'No one may disturb her.'

'Danny's right. We'll wake her up,' said Maddy, shrugging. 'Once she knows Liadan is stirring things up, she'll get everything back to normal.'

'But the Morrighan never wakes,' said Fionn.

'Never?' yelped Danny.

'Not since she left your world. I told you, she created the Land with her dreams, and it is her dreaming that keeps our world alive.'

'She NEVER wakes up?!' asked Maddy, incredulous. 'You're telling me she has been asleep for thousands of years?'

'Yes,' said Fionn.

'But how did she interfere in the war? How did she make Liadan a queen?' asked Roisin.

'If you cause ripples across her dream, as Liadan did, then the Morrighan's mind will turn toward you.' Fionn shuddered. 'That's not something you want.'

'It is, if it gets us out of here any quicker!' said Danny. 'So what do we have to do to make her notice us? Is what Liadan's doing not enough?'

'Not yet,' said Fionn sadly.

'Then we have to wake her,' said Maddy. 'This has already gone too far.'

'No one wakes the Morrighan!' said Fionn.

'But—' Roisin began.

'No one! Waking the Morrighan is not something anyone should do,' said Fionn, glaring at them before turning her back on them and marching off.

Maddy looked at Danny and Roisin, stunned at the anger shown by the normally timid little dryad. Roisin raised an eyebrow.

'It looks like there's no plan B,' said Danny, turning to follow Fionn.

chapter fourteen

The trees began to thin until they petered out to reveal a stony, snow-covered beach. A frozen lake lay still and quiet under the sullen weight of ice. The sun still peeked over the edge of the horizon, the dying light staining the surface of the ice with its blood.

Rising above the flat glass of the lake, the White Tower twisted and turned in on itself as it reached toward the sky. Fionn and the children clung to the bark of one of the trees that marked the boundary between the forest and the shore, hunched in its shadow. Maddy tucked her bare hands into her armpits and squinted into an icy wind that scoured her face and made her lungs burn with the cold.

If Liadan's home reflected her personality, Maddy was worried the Winter Queen was seriously nuts.

The base of the tower was nothing more than a jumble of caves tumbled upon one another. As Maddy's eyes rose up the rock face, a smooth tower began to form. But it also expanded, spreading out from its ugly base until it looked like it was defying gravity. Spiky little turrets shot off into the air from the main building like fireworks, growing more numerous as the structure spread. They also grew more decorative, until the very top ones were smothered in balconies cut into filigree patterns, statues and gargoyles and multi-paned windows that flashed in the evening rays.

It looked, Maddy decided, like a toy faerie-tale castle dreamed up by a small child with no taste, who then got bored and took a blowtorch to its plastic base.

It also looked completely deserted, which struck her as being more than a bit suspicious. She could imagine Liadan crouching like a spider in the middle of that mess of stone, waiting for them to come closer.

'How do we get there? I can't see a bridge,' said Danny.

'Liadan makes one from ice, but you'll have to walk,' said Fionn.

'You must be joking!' said Roisin. 'That ice could break under our weight. We'll drown.'

The dryad shrugged. 'No other way. I must stop here. I cannot go too far from my tree – it needs me.'

Danny walked to the edge of the shore and crouched down to sweep snow from the surface of the ice. 'It looks pretty thick,' he called back over his shoulder. 'I reckon we could walk across it.' He stood up and took a tentative step on to the ice, then another, and then he jumped up and down. The ice didn't make a sound or splinter.

The wind died suddenly. 'Thank goodness for that,' said Roisin. 'That wind was freezing.'

'OK, let's think about this,' said Maddy. 'We need to spread out in case something happens – that way at least one of us is more likely to get through.'

'What? In case one of us needs help?' said Roisin.

'We can all swim,' said Maddy. 'I've got the rucksack, so I'll go first. Roisin, you keep hold of George and give me a ten-minute head start. And Danny, you follow Roisin in another ten minutes. That way we spread our weight across the ice.'

'Do you really think that's going to help?' said Danny.

'It can't do any harm,' said Maddy.

Roisin tucked her jacket into the waistband of her jeans and pushed George inside, zipping it up so only his head was visible. Then they all turned to say goodbye to Fionn, who stood wringing her hands.

'Thank you, Fionn, for getting us this far,' said Maddy.

The dryad smiled. 'I'm glad I didn't hide in my tree,' she said. 'Walk fast and leave quickly. Then Winter will end.'

'We'll do our best,' said Danny.

Maddy took a tentative step on to the ice, then

another, and another, until she was moving gingerly across the lake's surface, her feet slipping underneath her as she walked.

'Try and step on drifts of snow. It will give your trainers something to grip,' Danny shouted from the shore.

'Ta very much, genius. I'll bear that in mind,' muttered Maddy through gritted teeth. She did not dare turn around in case she fell. Her legs were aching with the effort of trying to keep her balance. She wished there was a breeze now. She was feeling warm from the effort of walking on the ice, and sweat was beginning to bead on her face. The shadow of the tower reached out to her across the ice, splintering the rays of the hovering sun against its thick lower walls.

Suddenly Roisin screamed and Maddy nearly fell as she turned to see what was going on.

Fionn was running on to the ice, shouting and waving her arms. A long crack ran ahead of her silver feet, and the noise of the ice ripping apart tore through the air. Maddy's breath froze in her throat as she watched the crack reaching out for Danny, who was slipping and stumbling along just behind Roisin – too close. Maddy strained to hear what Fionn was shouting. Then the undergrowth in the forest behind the dryad shook and dark shapes burst from the trees and raced on to the ice. Wolves. Maddy screamed, her voice mingling with Roisin's and Danny's as the pack ran on, barking and yipping with excitement, their huge paws not troubled by the slippery surface. Three silvery grey wolves were running at the head of the pack. Maddy watched, frozen, as they caught up with Danny and pounced, pulling him on to his back. He shouted and struggled and staggered back to his feet, but they locked their jaws on to his wrists and clothing and started to drag him back to shore. Maddy watched in horror as he fell to his knees and tried to beat them off with his fists. He punched one animal in the snout and it backed off for a second, its lips curled in a snarl, before it lunged forward, sank its teeth into his jacket and dragged him along. Five more were bounding across the ice toward Roisin, who stood with her arms wrapped around George. 'MADDY! DON'T LEAVE ME, MADDY!' she screamed in terror. Maddy started to run, her trainers slithering on the glassy surface of the ice, slowing her down. As she strained to reach Roisin, the wolves surrounded her and Roisin went down among the furry bodies.

Maddy cried out in horror as Roisin struggled in among the pack. She could see the white soles of her cousin's trainers flash as she kicked out at the wolves' legs, one arm wrapped around her head and the other holding George tight to her chest. The animals sidestepped her kicks neatly, their paws dancing as nimbly as ballerinas.

Then Maddy saw a wolf run away from Roisin and head straight for her, followed by some of the pack. The leader was the big black male who had attacked them earlier, his eyes glowing with green fire and his fur flecked with saliva, his red tongue lolling from between his teeth. His eyes locked on Maddy and he put on a burst of speed.

Panicked, Maddy tried to run faster toward Roisin, but she slipped and fell face first on to the ice. Blood gushed from her nose and she choked as the hot, salty liquid filled the back of her throat. The ice groaned and cracks shot out around her spreadeagled body, and as she tried to get to her feet, her knee went through the ice. She watched transfixed as icy water spread like a stain through the denim of her jeans. Beneath the palms of her hands, tiny cracks spread lazily. She fixed her eyes on them and tried to calm her breathing. Blood roared in her ears, but she could still hear the pack bearing down on her. The thud of their paws on the ice advanced each crack by a millimetre, and their excited growls rasped the frosty air. She had to move or they would scoop her off the ice and rip her apart between them as easily as a rabbit.

Gently she lifted her knee from the hole. The ice

creaked and skittered beneath her. She slowly got to her feet, as the cracks began to flake and yawn wide. She tensed her calf muscles, hoping to leap clear of the damaged ice, but it was too late – the whole lot gave way beneath her just as she felt the breath of the black wolf blast her face and she fell into the icy waters.

The cold drove the breath from her lungs and she gasped, swallowing water as she thrashed about in panic. The current grabbed her and started to tug her away from the hole in the ice. Desperately, she gripped the edge of the hole with fingers that felt like sausages. The freezing water tore at her savagely, making her muscles judder with pain. Above her, the wolves milled excitedly, blocking out the last of the daylight and casting her into darkness. She couldn't climb out into their waiting jaws, but her body was succumbing to the cold. Numbness began to creep over her and she struggled to move her legs to tread water.

She was also running out of air – her lungs burned and black spots danced in front of her eyes. She lifted her head to take a breath, keeping as much of her face underwater as she could while the wolves scrabbled at the edges of the ice with their paws, making the hole bigger. Maddy was relieved that she wouldn't be sucked under the ice, but now she couldn't kick her legs with any power and she began to feel her frozen body sink into the depths as her useless fingers lost their grip on the ice. She cried out as the big black male sank his head under the water, closed his jaws around her neck and pulled her up on to the surface. She screamed with pain and, as more teeth bit down on her arms, she sobbed with fear, dreading the agony when they would start to rip her apart. She tried to curl up, to protect herself from their jaws, her skin red raw from the cold. But instead they dragged her face down across the ice as it cracked around them like gunshots, all the way back to the rocky shore, where they let her lie down to cough blood and mucus on to the snow.

She stared at the wolf's paws in front of her. He made no move to attack her and she twisted in pain as her numb body began to warm up again. The pack whined and yipped around her and she got to her hands and knees. She shook uncontrollably with cold as she vomited in the snow. She glared at the black wolf as he cocked his head to one side.

'You don't seem much of a big bad wolf to me,' she mumbled through blue lips. The animal narrowed his eyes and laid his ears flat against his head. She tried to tense herself for his spring, but her exhausted shaking muscles didn't listen.

'You're no Red Riding Hood yourself,' said the wolf.

chapter fifteen

Maddy sank down into the snow, too tired to care about the wolf talking to her, and curled in on herself for warmth. She clamped her teeth against the painful spasms in her body and closed her eyes. *I'll try to sleep*, she thought. *I'll deal with all this when I feel a bit better*.

Sharp little hands dug into her sodden clothes and yanked her to her feet. Fionn was there, struggling with the zip on Maddy's coat and crying, bright green tears glistening on her face.

'My fault, my fault,' she sobbed. 'The air was getting warmer, but I was scared, so scared, and my tree was calling me. I went away, and when I came back it was too late! Fenris saved you instead, good Fenris!'

Relief pricked sharp through the fug of tiredness that cocooned Maddy's brain. The wolves had been helping. She was not about to be dinner.

'Who's Fenris?' mumbled Maddy, as Fionn yanked

her stiffening jumper and T-shirt over her head. The black wolf looked at her disdainfully. 'Oh. Right. Why are you taking my clothes, Fionn?'

The dryad yanked Maddy's jeans around her ankles and pulled her forward into an awkward hop. 'Your clothes are freezing on to you, and you'll get very sick if you don't get out of them. Liadan did this. She can't touch you herself, but she can make the weather harm you. She warmed the ice on the lake enough to make it dangerous, and now the temperature has dropped again – can't you feel it?'

Maddy stood in her bare feet in the snow. 'Actually, no. I'm feeling much better now – a bit warmer. Very sleepy though.'

'That's bad,' said Fenris, as Fionn pushed Maddy toward a knot of wolves lying among the trees. Roisin and Danny's pale faces gleamed up at her from a swirl of grey, brown and cream fur. Fionn pushed Maddy down and the knot contracted around her, sucking her deep into the warm soft mass to float beside her cousins.

When Maddy woke up the first thing she smelt was damp dog and the first thing she felt was the pain in her face and hands. Her whole body hurt, but her scraped and bloodied fingers screamed the loudest as she tried to uncurl them. Her nose and lips felt huge. The wolves were a breathing wall of fur around her and they were wrapped around each other so tight it was hard to see where one wolf started and another ended. That is, apart from one pair of green eyes that were beginning to look familiar.

'Sleep well?' asked the black wolf.

'I might have slept better if you hadn't dragged me around on my face,' she mumbled through bruised lips.

'We did not have time for finesse or a more dignified return to shore,' said Fenris. 'However, I still think "thank you" would be the gracious thing to say, rather than a complaint about the service.'

'I'll thank you when I know why you saved us,' said Maddy.

The wolf growled and bared his teeth. Feeling his mood, the pack began to unravel, leaving Maddy shivering in the snow. As some of the animals stood up, her clothes dropped from their backs and stomachs, warm and dry and smelling to high heaven of the sharp, wild scent of wolf.

She grabbed them and dressed herself quickly. Danny, Roisin and Fionn got up too, bleary-eyed. George was stiff with fear and looked as if he had not slept a wink. The pack gathered behind Fenris, who lowered his shaggy head and glared fiercely at Maddy.

'What's happening?' said Fionn, yawning.

'It seems that our help is not appreciated and we made a mistake when we saved your friends,' he growled.

'No, we appreciate it,' said Roisin quickly. 'It's just that . . . well . . . you know . . .' She wilted under Fenris's baleful stare.

'It's just that you attacked us in the forest,' said Danny. 'Which makes us worry about why you helped us now.'

'We know you belong to the Winter Queen – everyone calls you the wolves of the White Tower,' said Maddy. 'She just tried to drown us, so it's a bit weird that you guys came to the rescue.'

The wolves stood so still there hardly seemed to be a breath shared among them. They looked at Maddy with their long eyes. Another moment and she knew they would melt back among the trees. Some gesture needed to be made, a word said, that would smooth the raised hackles on Fenris's broad back, but she did not have a clue what to do.

It was Fionn who broke the silence. 'They are only saplings,' she said to the wolves. 'There is a world of things they don't know.'

'Can *you* not trust in a good deed?' growled Fenris.

Fionn shrugged. 'You're not faerie,' she said. 'I don't know you.'

A silver-coloured female, her belly swollen with pregnancy, glided up to Fenris and rubbed her face against his. She nuzzled his ear and the tension went out of his huge body. He sat down in the snow and leaned into the female's shoulder.

'I am Nitaina, the story keeper of my pack,' the female said. 'We were of your world once,' she explained to Maddy. 'We came from a fertile land of tall grasses and herds of beasts for plentiful food. We shared it with humans too and we lived in peace – there was territory enough for all. But then new humans came, with pale, hairy faces, and the herds grew more scarce. We decided to leave, to head north to the ice lands where we could live away from people. One night, when we were trying to slip by a wooden mountain that the new men slept in, we got lost in a snowstorm. We couldn't hear or see anything; we could smell only each other. We lay down and huddled together to wait for the storm to pass. When we woke up, we were here. The Winter Queen offered us sanctuary, if we became her eyes and ears.' The wolf lifted her head and looked down her long nose at them. 'But we do not belong to her. We are free, and our will is our own.'

Maddy shuffled her feet and felt embarrassed to meet Nitaina's cool, proud stare. Her soft, clear voice and the knowledge that she had risked her unborn pups on the melting ice made her feel ashamed of quarrelling with the wolves. But something about the answer still bothered her.

'I am sorry that your tribe has suffered, I really am,' she said, 'but you still haven't explained why you went to so much trouble for us.'

'We have seen the children the Winter Queen has tired of,' Nitaina said. 'They slip away from the tower and they wander the forest with their minds broken. They are ugly, feral things, cast out from their own kind.' She looked at Fenris, who lowered his shaggy head to the ground and sighed. 'It is not right,' she said to him softly. 'We know it is not right.'

She turned back to the children. 'Young ones should be with their mothers. We have heard you are seeking a young child, to bring him home. I will not stand by to watch another child broken. We are the Amaguk tribe, and while we may be exiles, we still know what is right and what is wrong.'

'That's all great, but I've got teeth marks in my arm from one of you lot,' said Danny. 'If you're so noble, then how come you sneak around playing story-book wolves?'

A shaggy grey wolf glided up to Danny. His eyes glinted, and as his tongue lolled from his mouth he looked as if he was laughing. He cocked his head and examined Danny's torn sleeve. 'I could have sworn I got a better hold than that,' he said.

'That was you?' said Danny.

The wolf bowed his head. 'Nero, at your service.'

'You could have had my arm off!' said Danny.

'Mmmm, if I'd wanted to,' said Nero. 'Rather remiss of me. Shall I have another go?'

Danny scowled at him.

'How are your ribs?' asked Maddy cheerfully.

The wolf's teeth snapped shut and he didn't look like he was laughing any more. 'Sore, as a matter of fact,' he growled.

'That makes us even then,' said Maddy.

'Um, thank you anyway,' said Roisin, as Nero and Maddy eyed each other. She looked at Fenris. 'Honestly, thank you.' He inclined his shaggy head in acknowledgement.

'Have you seen Stephen?' asked Maddy.

'Yes,' said Nitaina. 'He passed through here with the Winter Queen and a hunting party. He slept in her arms as she rode by.' She looked at Maddy. 'He was very pale. You need to find him quickly.'

'Is there any way to get into the White Tower other than across the lake?' asked Danny.

'No way by land . . .' said Fionn.

'But there is a way, right?' said Danny.

Fionn twisted her hands and looked about her.

'Fionn?'

'Only one way to get to the tower now.'

'And?' snapped Maddy.

'You fly.'

'Of course,' said Maddy. 'And how are we supposed to do that?'

Fionn looked at the wolves nervously. Their gimlet eyes stared back at her, but they didn't make a sound.

'There is a faerie, a strange one, in the mountains, who could help you,' said Fionn.

'How is she strange? Doesn't like doing nasty things to people, does she?' asked Roisin.

'No, lives on her own too much, gone a bit rotten in the head,' said Fionn. 'Too many squirrels nesting upstairs. If the Amaguks bring you to the foot of the Skyring, a mountain range just a little beyond the tower, you'll find her.'

Maddy narrowed her eyes at her. 'Why – where are you going?'

'Home,' said Fionn, as she wrung her hands. 'I need to go to my tree. Need to sleep. Tree is already sick, won't last long if I stay away.'

'Please don't, Fionn,' pleaded Roisin. 'We can't do this on our own. You said it yourself – we nearly died on the ice, and we only made it this far thanks to you. You can't leave us now.'

'No,' said Fionn, shaking her head. 'Liadan will see. She knows everything.'

'But if we don't help Stephen and break Liadan's grip, then Summer will never come – you said so yourself,' said Danny. 'What will happen to the forest then?'

'We will live to see Summer,' said Fionn, as she backed away from them. 'There will always be trees.'

'I don't reckon this weirdo faerie is going to help us unless another faerie speaks for us,' said Danny. 'No offence to the Amaguks, but the locals seem to be as suspicious of them as they are of us. I don't see how we are going to make it without you, Fionn.'

But the little dryad just shook her head and continued to back away.

'Wait, Fionn,' said Maddy. 'Can't you do this for Stephen?'

'My tree needs me,' she said.

'I know, but . . . think about it,' said Maddy, struggling to keep the desperation from her voice as she watched Fionn's eyes dart around. 'You were so pleased that you were doing something. You knew you were helping your tree when you helped us. Do you remember?'

Fionn nodded, her eyes wary. But she stopped sidling away.

'You were so brave when you helped us,' Maddy continued, her voice soft. She was pleased to see a green blush stealing through Fionn's cheeks. 'Stephen means as much to me as your tree does to you. But he can't last as long on his own. He's already been away from home for much too long. He's not even a sapling – he's a tiny, tiny little seedling. You know how fragile they are, don't you?'

Fionn nodded. Her body looked tense but her head was cocked to the sound of Maddy's voice. 'So many bad things happen to seedlings,' she said. 'Animals eat them, elves crush them. That's why they need their dryad.'

'I know, I know,' said Maddy. 'Only Stephen doesn't have a dryad; he's got a mum, back in our world. She can't come in here, and he can't get out without us. Can you imagine how much danger he is in? What his mother is going through? Can you imagine if you were locked away from your tree?'

Fionn shuddered.

'You were brave to help your tree, but if you help Stephen, you'll be more than brave,' said Maddy. 'You'll be doing something pure and good and noble because you'll be doing it for someone else. You'll be a hero.'

Fionn didn't say anything but Maddy was sure that she saw her stand a little straighter and puff her chest out a little as she thought about this.

'And I'll keep you safe from Liadan,' said Danny. He walked over to the little dryad and took her tiny hand in his. 'I promise I won't let anyone hurt you because you helped Stephen.'

Fionn blushed a deep emerald as she looked up at Danny and sighed. 'All right, I'll help your seedling,' she said, gazing into his eyes.

CHAPTER SIXTEEN

Fionn practically danced away through the trees, her silver hair shining bright as a new star as it swirled around her. The little dryad glowed as she flitted back and forth between Danny and the path ahead. Her soft voice rustled through the air like leaves playing in the breeze as she whispered and laughed with him, her tiny thin hands patting him now and then.

Roisin walked next to Maddy as the wolves drifted around them. 'Do you think Fionn fancies Danny?' she asked, as she stared at the pair in amazement.

Maddy raised her eyebrows. 'Oh yes!'

They looked at each other and burst out laughing, clapping their hands to their mouths to smother their giggles when Danny looked back at them with a frown on his face.

He opened his mouth to say something, but Fionn distracted him by tugging on his hands.

'Imagine anyone fancying Danny!' said Roisin. 'Yuck!'

'Fair play to him though,' said Maddy. 'He said just the right thing back there.'

'I know. I'm still in shock,' said Roisin. 'Danny being diplomatic for once. I didn't think he had it in him. I thought he was going to hit her until she said yes. It's what he always does to me.'

'I don't think he was being diplomatic,' said Maddy. She dropped her voice to a throaty whisper and wiggled her eyebrows dramatically. 'I think he was being *seductive*.'

Roisin nearly choked on her laugh and Maddy started giggling again until a low growl from Fenris warned them to be quiet. Danny shot them both a filthy look. Maddy hoped he hadn't heard.

They hadn't been walking for long when they came to a cleared area of forest that had been fenced off into paddocks. The wolves flattened themselves into the grass. White horses stood around in the paddocks, their bodies alert and their ears pricked toward the tower. Fionn hunkered down, the long grass brushing her upturned nose, and pulled Danny down beside her.

'Get down,' she hissed at Maddy and Roisin. 'Time to be mice again.'

'What's going on?' asked Maddy.

'We're going to wait in the trees for a while,' said Fenris. 'The elven mounts are dangerous. If they see us, they might jump the fence to give chase, and I'm not risking the pack. We need to get past when they have been fed and are sleepy.'

'They're only horses,' said Danny. 'Let's go past now – who cares if they see us?'

Fionn waved a long hand and blinked slowly at him. 'Not horses, very dangerous.'

Danny looked again. 'They look like horses to me.'

Roisin gazed at the paddocks and the animals that littered the green grass like statues, a frown puckering the skin between her eyebrows. 'They're not grazing,' she said after a minute.

Fionn nodded her head. 'They don't eat grass – they eat meat. Watch.'

They all flattened themselves on the ground as they saw lights approaching through the trees ahead. As the sounds of singing drifted toward them, the wolves melted into the shadows and lidded their eyes so they wouldn't reflect in the lights.

A group of elves appeared from the trees, some of them dragging a wooden cart covered in a rough brown cloth. The metallic scent of blood filled the air and the elven mounts rushed to the far fence and milled about, snorting and prancing. Maddy could only imagine what the smell of blood was doing to the wolves, whose wet noses were quivering. The elves reached the fence and threw back the cloth, revealing a heap of raw meat. They began to throw it over the fence at the animals, who reared up and pawed the air. They snapped at gobbets of flesh, before wheeling around to tear at them on the ground. As they ripped and chewed, Maddy could see they were things out of a nightmare – huge yellowed fangs curled in their mouths, while their feet ended not in hoofs, but in paws with wicked claws.

A small female, chased off the carcasses by her bigger companions, snapped her fangs at the elves, her ears flattened against her skull. One elf, his clothes streaked with blood, got too close the fence and she reared, lashing out at him with her front legs. The elf screamed and staggered backwards, clutching his arm, blood welling up between his fingers, while his companions laughed. He swore at the female, who neighed and bared her teeth, her eyes red with rage. The children lay and listened to the sounds of teeth and claws ripping and tearing, long after the elves had disappeared back up the path.

Afterwards, their gleaming white hides splattered and smeared with blood, the mounts lay down to sleep off their meal. The little female picked over the remains of the carcasses, crunching bones for their marrow. Now and then, a sound in the surrounding forest or the movement of some small and frightened creature would catch her attention and her head would jerk up and her mean red eyes scan the trees while her lips peeled back from her fangs.

'We wait,' whispered Fionn. 'Elven mounts are not going to let a stranger slip past – you can't bribe them with an apple.'

The children nodded, dumb with fear, and crept back into the trees with the Amaguks to discuss tactics. 'We're hungry, and there is plenty of meat left scattered in those paddocks,' said Nitaina. 'Some of the pack will go in and carry out the leftovers. The mounts won't like it, but they are used to our scent and will leave us be. Later, when they sleep, we will slip past them, with you three crawling on your hands and knees among us. Our scent is on your clothing so they will not pick you out from among us and raise the alarm. We have all been walking for a long time, so I suggest we get some sleep while we wait.'

A few of the pack slipped away with Fenris to brave the paddock while the rest curled around Nitaina. Fionn followed Danny to sit at the base of a bald oak tree. She wrapped her thin arms around one of his, leaned her head against his shoulder and closed her eyes. Danny sat

stiff and awkward, glaring at Maddy and Roisin, daring
them with his eyes to say something.

Maddy sat on the cold forest floor next to Roisin,
who had her arms clasped around her knees and her
face tilted up to the turquoise sky, where a few stars had
begun to twinkle in the shadowy edges of the sky's bowl.
George was curled against her feet, his belly rising and
falling with deep breaths, his paws paddling as he chased
rabbits in his sleep. Maddy put her head in her hands
and tried to relax. But the fear she had been living with
ever since they had stepped through the mound was
still humming through her and she knew she would not
be able to sleep. She thought of the tower, its unnatural
stillness as she had inched her way toward it over the ice.
Nothing had moved in the light-filled rooms, no sounds
had drifted through the air, but it still felt full of life.
Teeming, evil, alert life. She had felt a thousand minds,
leaning forward in the tower, focusing in on her single
heartbeat as she struggled on the frozen surface of the
lake. Fionn had told them to be like mice. Fachtna had
called them insects. Maddy had never felt so small, so
lost, even when she was told her parents were dead.

She sneaked a glance at Roisin and was surprised to
see a small smile hovering on her lips. She looked happy
and peaceful. The shadows from the trees lay velvety on
her face, staining the closed lids of her eyes and her lips

almost black. Maddy felt a spasm of guilt. She realized Roisin was the only one of her cousins who had ever actually tried to be friends.

'I'm really sorry, Ro,' she whispered.

'Hmmm?' said Roisin, opening her eyes and blinking at Maddy sleepily. 'What for?'

'For dragging you into all this,' said Maddy.

'Don't be,' said Roisin. 'I'm glad I'm here. Well, the threat of death is a bit of a pain, and I'd kill for a burger and chips, but how many people get to see the Land of Eternal Youth?'

Maddy stared at her, open-mouthed. 'Roisin,' she said, 'this place is a hellhole.'

Roisin laughed. 'It's not, you know. It's really not. We've been so scared and we've been on the run pretty much ever since we set foot in here so we haven't had time to look around us. Remember how we felt when we first opened our eyes? This place is the dream of a faerie, Maddy. Forget about Liadan, just for a second, and listen.'

Maddy sat and listened and tried to figure out what Roisin meant. At first all she could hear was the sound of the forest around them, the rustle of small warm bodies creeping through the undergrowth, the creak of the trees as their topmost branches swayed in the breeze.

And then she heard it. That strange singing that had been there in the background ever since they stepped off the mound, now getting stronger as night fell. There were no words to the song, just high, sweet notes that trembled and ached at the very highest reach of her hearing. It swooped and trilled and soared with such joy that Maddy felt her own heart grow lighter as she listened to it.

'Who's singing ?' she whispered to Roisin, her own voice thick with tears of happiness.

Roisin slipped a hand into Maddy's. 'Look up,' she whispered.

Maddy tilted her face to the darkening sky. The sun had finally sunk beneath the horizon, its last rays pale against the dark land. The sky had turned a deep sapphire blue and the stars were shining boldly now. One in particular stood out bigger and brighter than the rest, and as Maddy watched its celestial light throbbed and pulsed with the rise and fall of the song. She felt a thrill of surprise going through her and she squeezed Roisin's hand. Roisin squeezed back and laughed softly.

'See?' said Roisin. 'The stars really do sing here.'

'They do,' said Maddy. 'I just hope Cernunnos can slow time enough for us to make it home. I don't want to listen to them sing forever.'

CHAPTER SEVENTEEN

Maddy must have dozed off at some point, because she was woken by a pain in her neck from lying on the forest floor and George licking her face. A full moon hung bloated above them and bathed the ground in silvery light. She disentangled her hand from Roisin's and climbed stiffly to her feet, an excited George bouncing around her. Icy leaf litter crunched under the rubber soles of her trainers. Sleepy birds crooned as they huddled together on the snow-crusted branches. Now and then an eye blinked at her from the rough bark. Small childlike shapes scampered away from her, swallowed up in an inkling by the dark beneath the trees.

The wolves were pacing and stretching. Nitaina heaved her pregnant body upright, shaking grass from her thick grey coat. Roisin stumbled along behind her, rubbing her eyes, while Danny was patiently listening to a twittering, twitching Fionn.

Fenris growled when he saw her. 'At last. I thought I was going to have to bite you to make you wake up,' he said.

'Keep your fur on,' said Maddy. 'We can't have been sleeping that long.' She grabbed a wriggling George and clipped the lead to his collar.

'We need to get moving,' said Roisin. 'We have no idea how long we've been here. My mam is going to be going mental.'

'Nothing new there,' muttered Maddy.

'I heard that,' said Danny, narrowing his eyes at her.

'You will all have to crawl through the grass so the mounts don't see you,' said Fenris, as the pack gathered. 'We'll surround you so they will keep their eyes on us. Move quickly and quietly.'

Maddy curled George's lead tight around her hand and patted him on the head. He was very slowly getting used to the wolves, but he was still tense and cautious. 'Be a good boy,' she whispered.

They reached the edge of the trees and Maddy could see the elven mounts in the paddock. Most of them were sprawled on the grass, dozing, their gleaming white hides still spattered with blood and gore from their meal. As the moon rose higher in the sky, it turned their faces black where their muzzles had been dipped in blood. Their lips twitched back from their fangs as they dreamed, while the littlest mare slept on her feet, her nose on her chest, slightly apart from the rest of the herd.

Maddy felt ill just looking at them. Danny turned a white face to her. 'I want a poker in my hand, going past that lot,' he whispered.

She nodded and carefully opened the rucksack, peeling the zip back slowly. Danny gripped a poker between two hands so it wouldn't clank against its partner as he pulled it out. Maddy took the other one and decided to bury the bag under a pile of leaves. There were only a few biscuits left, and she didn't want anything to slow her down as they sneaked past the mounts.

'Are you finally ready?' asked Fenris. Maddy nodded. 'Then let's go. And remember, move quickly.'

The pack formed a tight knot around them as Maddy, Roisin, Danny and Fionn lay on their bellies and began to squirm forward on their elbows through the long meadow grass, skirting the edge of the paddock. Maddy's clothes were quickly soaked, and the grass was tickling her nose. George stopped and started as her arm swept forward and back like a swimmer's with his lead clutched firmly in her fist, but the little terrier didn't utter a sound.

Maddy didn't realize how scared she was until she felt her breath catching in her chest in short, shallow gulps. She was using her wrists to try to keep the poker and George's lead from dragging on the ground and her arms had begun to ache within seconds. She paused for a moment to slow her heart and take deeper breaths. The wolves halted around her and she felt sharp teeth nip the back of her knee. *OK, OK*, she thought. She had just started to crawl again when she felt the wolves freeze.

Then she heard it. The slow, even rhythm of feet padding toward them.

She held her breath and turned her head to the left to look at the paddock fence. Between the wolves' legs she could see a mount's clawed feet as it walked up to the fence. A muzzle dropped down and she watched the huge nostrils flare and collapse, flare and collapse as the animal sucked in lungfuls of air, searching for their scent. Maddy saw the nose disappear and then heard the high, enraged whinny. The wolves surged forward. 'Run!' barked Fenris.

Maddy scooped George up under her arm and scrambled to her feet, her trainers slipping on the wet grass. She raced for the trees on the far side of the clearing, the wolves' rear guard herding her forward. Danny, Fionn and Roisin were ahead of her, arms and legs pumping. Roisin was the first to reach the trees, but instead of running on, she turned to look back and her mouth became a small O of fear.

Maddy knew she shouldn't, but at the sound of splintering wood behind them she had to turn to see what Roisin was looking at. The little female had smashed part of the high fence down and jumped it. Now she was galloping toward them, clumps of turf flying up from her feet, her neck stretched out and her eyes blazing with hate. Her snapping fangs were virtually on Nero's tail as he raced for the trees.

We can't outrun her, Maddy thought. She stood rooted to the spot as she watched the mare bear down on Nero. She held George tight against her chest, the little terrier's heart pounding against her palm. Tears pricked her eyes as she watched the grey wolf bunch his muscles for one last, desperate surge and she yelled a warning as the mare's teeth raked his hindquarters. Nero staggered and went down, a blur of grey fur and snapping teeth, as the mare screeched and lunged at him, her claws raking him as he struggled to get up. Two of the pack saw he was in trouble and bent their bodies double to turn back and face the mount, their huge paws crossing daintily as they struggled to keep up their speed. A black shadow blurred past Maddy. It was Fenris, hackles up, racing to the fight.

The wolves leaped and latched on to the mount's neck and hindquarters, trying desperately to bring her down. She bucked and reared and lashed out with her talons, fresh blood staining her coat, flinging the wolves against the ground as fast as they got a hold on her and trampling them with her feet. The pack were fighting hard, but Maddy could see that they were only slowing the mount down.

Without thinking she put George on the ground and charged into the fight, dimly hearing Danny and Roisin yelling behind her. For a split second she wondered what the hell she was doing as the mount shook off Fenris and spun to face her. Her feet were out of control and she slammed into the mare's bloodstained chest so hard she nearly bounced off it to the ground. She grabbed a hank of long mane to keep her upright as the mount rolled her maddened eyes and bared her fangs, the stink of her breath rolling over Maddy's face as she stabbed up with the dull point of the poker. She heard the mount roar with pain and saw the iron pierce the soft flesh at her throat. The mount reared and brought her front legs up sharply, thumping Maddy hard in the chest and knocking her off her feet. Then she raised a leg, spread her claws and slashed down, ripping through Maddy's jacket and tearing the skin on her back as she tried to roll away. Maddy screamed as red-hot pain lanced across her spine, and rolled again as the mount slammed a taloned paw into the earth where her head had been just a split second earlier. She tried to back away on all fours, but the mare whipped her head around, jaws gaping, and went for her face.

Maddy closed her eyes just before someone slammed into her from the side, causing the pain in her back to flare up into agony. She tumbled over in the wet grass as Danny got to his feet and pulled her up with him, his poker held out in front of him. Just as the mount went to lunge again, a little streak of silver sped past them. It was Fionn, who danced right up to the mount's nose.

'Stupid horsey,' she squeaked, waving her twiggy arms in the mount's face. 'Come and get me.'

Maddy watched in horror as the mount spun and focused on the little dryad. The wolves circled cautiously, waiting for a chance to pounce.

'She's going to make firewood out of Fionn,' gasped Maddy.

'No, she's not,' said Danny grimly, hefting his poker and charging at the mount.

'Stay close to her!' Roisin yelled as Danny ran to help Fionn. 'Stay close to her shoulder and she can't kick or bite you!'

Danny could not have heard Roisin properly, because he ran up to the mount, grabbed a handful of mane and hauled himself on to her back.

'What are you doing?!' shrieked Roisin. 'I never said anything about riding her!'

'I'm getting her away from you!' yelled Danny. He kicked his feet against her sides. 'Giddy up!'

For a moment Maddy thought it would work. For a moment the mount froze, her ears flicking back as training took over from instinct and she listened to what her rider demanded. The she remembered who her rider was, bunched her muscles and bucked hard.

Danny tried desperately to hang on as Roisin, Maddy and Fionn screamed. He fell forward as the mount's hind feet came up, dropping the poker and wrapping his arms around her neck. She bucked again and Danny shouted as he was catapulted through the air. As he crashed to the ground, she turned back to where Maddy and Roisin huddled together. Fionn ran to them and crouched next to Maddy. Behind the mount, the pack saw their chance and tensed to spring.

This is it, thought Maddy. She slowly got to her feet and adjusted her grip on the poker as the mount stalked toward them. *When she attacks, I'm going to shove this right down her throat . . . and hope she doesn't rip my face off first.*

Then something large flew over Maddy's head. She ducked and blinked as a faerie landed in front of the mount, throwing its hand out. There was a flash of silver and the mount reared and crashed to her knees, sinking forward on to her face, before slowly collapsing over on one side. Maddy stared in shock as the mare's hate-filled eyes dulled and turned glassy, her blood steaming in the frigid air as it poured from around the blade sticking into her throat.

A bone-white hand covered in grey tattoos bent to pull the knife from the mount's cooling flesh.

'Well, well, well,' said a rasping voice. 'What do we have here?'

Maddy swallowed as her eyes met a familiar blood-red gaze.

Fachtna.

CHAPTER EIGHTEEN

Fachtna's gauzy wings settled like a cloud about her shoulders as she plunged her knife into the earth to clean the mount's blood from its silver blade. She rose and strode toward Maddy, the various knives strapped around her body chinking sweetly.

Maddy braced herself, but Fachtna swept past to stand in front of Roisin and Fionn, raising her wings so that a dark shadow fell upon them. Fionn trembled and wrapped her arms around Roisin's waist, hiding her face against her shoulder. Roisin tried to edge around Fachtna and back to Maddy, her arms tight around Fionn, but Fachtna grabbed a handful of Roisin's jacket and rooted her to the spot.

'Look at me,' she commanded, but Fionn just shook her head and cried louder. Fachtna snarled, baring her shark's teeth, and reached down to grab Fionn by the hair.

To Maddy's horror, Roisin threw her arm up and grabbed Fachtna's wrist. 'Leave her alone,' she said.

Fachtna hissed and twisted her arm, breaking Roisin's grip. She moved so fast Maddy didn't have time to see or hear the knife being drawn from its sheath. The next thing she knew, Roisin was being forced to tilt her head back as the tip of a silver blade dimpled the skin at her throat, drawing a trickle of dark red blood.

'Did you think this was a game, little girl?' asked Fachtna, her voice soft in the silence. 'Did you think you could come here and play the hero, that you would dance with me around the toadstools before going home?'

With her free hand she grabbed Fionn by the hair. The dryad had wrapped her twiggy arms around Roisin's waist and tried to hang on, crying piteously, but Fachtna ripped her away and lifted her up to swing her in the air before her face.

Fionn clapped her hands over her eyes, but Fachtna shook her until the dryad's limbs jerked and flailed and she was forced to meet the faerie's baleful red glare.

'Treacherous little creature,' roared Fachtna. 'Did you think Queen Liadan would not know you had helped these mortals break a contract? What life for you, dryad, now that you have angered my queen?'

'Mercy,' sobbed Fionn, as she dangled from Fachtna's talons. 'Mercy! My tree . . . it is dying!'

'Let her go!'

Danny stood behind Fachtna, the poker back in his hand. The pack were gathering behind him silently, their rangy bodies hesitant and wary.

'I said, "Let her go,"' said Danny through clenched teeth. 'You're not touching her or any of my family.'

Fachtna's lip curled with contempt and she flung Fionn to the ground. She glanced at Danny, reversed the knife in her hand and then hit him between the eyes with its hilt, sending him sprawling backwards, where he lay dazed. Then she bent over the weeping dryad, the knife gleaming in her hand.

'A taste of what is to come,' Fachtna said, as she grabbed Fionn's wrist. The little dryad screamed as Fachtna brought her knife down on Fionn's outstretched fingers, severing two of them. Fionn's green blood splattered on to the snow. She dangled the howling dryad by her wrist and smiled at Maddy.

'Come save your friend,' taunted Fachtna.

Maddy's legs shook with fear. Roisin began to cry softly.

'No?' said Fachtna, arching a pale eyebrow in mock surprise. 'You would have her risk all for you and yet you will not take a step to save her? Perhaps I can persuade you to move.' She moved her knife toward Fionn's twiggy digits, as the dryad began to shriek in terror and twist in Fachtna's grip.

'NO!' yelled Maddy.

'Ah, you speak,' sneered Fachtna. 'Come then, fight me for your friend. Be as brave as that weakling boy.'

But Maddy couldn't. Her mind was blank with fear and it could not tell her legs to move.

Fachtna stared at her and gave a bark of laughter, before dropping Fionn and wiping her knife on her thigh. The dryad sobbed and shook with pain and terror, her maimed hand curled against her chest.

'You have condemned your tree to death,' said Fachtna. 'Go from this place and await your punishment.'

With a wail, Fionn scrambled to her feet and ran from the clearing without a backwards glance. The trees soon swallowed her up, but her sobs could still be heard. Fachtna turned to face the Amaguks, who cowered behind Fenris and Nitaina. The two leader wolves faced Fachtna with their heads held high and proud, but their eyes were tight with anxiety.

'Queen Liadan is most disappointed with you,' said Fachtna. 'She gave you sanctuary, and in return she thought she commanded your love, unswerving loyalty and unstinting devotion. You have proved her wrong. The Winter Queen does not like being told she is wrong.'

Nitaina opened her mouth to say something, but Fachtna cut her off. 'Silence!' she said. 'I do not wish to hear feeble excuses. Be grateful Queen Liadan does not feel you have outlived your usefulness, or else I would happily turn you and your unborn pups into rugs. Go now, and let her finish her game undisturbed.'

Nitaina looked at Maddy with sad eyes and then the wolves turned and slunk away. Danny climbed awkwardly to his feet and joined Maddy and Roisin, his palm pressed to his forehead. A trickle of blood seeped through his fingers. Fachtna's head turned to follow his every movement, her eyes unblinking. Maddy shuddered as her red gaze settled on her. George slunk behind Maddy's legs and bared his teeth at the faerie.

'If the choice was mine I would gut you and leave you for the crows,' said Fachtna. 'But luckily for you, Queen Liadan is merciful and is minded to give you another chance to finish the game. But if you try to get another faerie to help you, I will slice them open from belly to throat in front of you. Now, start walking.'

Numb with shock and the throbbing pain in her back, Maddy stumbled along, barely aware of how she managed to put one foot in front of the other. Danny's face was white and drawn, while Roisin tried to hush a growling, furious George, who bounced about at the end of his lead, trying to whip his stubby body about so he could face Fachtna.

Silent and grim, she herded them back the way they had come, past the mounts' paddocks, where the creatures cowered away from the smell of their mate's death, back through the hushed forest, its evergreen boughs shutting off the silvery light of the moon. Fachtna stalked through the gloaming like an angel of death, her body gleaming wherever slivers of moonlight could penetrate the canopy.

Maddy could have wept with despair and exhaustion as the trees began to thin out and she could hear the half-frozen lake throwing itself repeatedly on the rocky shore.

Fachtna pushed and harried them on to the beach. The icy wind that whipped off the waves froze Maddy's eyeballs dry, and she shivered as it forced its way through her clothes to chill her skin.

'Your deception means that the queen can impose further conditions on your bargain,' said Fachtna. Roisin opened her mouth to protest but Fachtna cut her off. 'Be grateful. You broke the terms of the contract and my queen is now free of her oath. I could kill you where you stand, and the child is hers to do with as she wishes. Yet the game plays on.

'Queen Liadan has decreed that there is no way

for you to reach the White Tower except by water,' she continued. 'You may not go back into the forest and seek help from others. And this time she is making sure you keep to the conditions.'

Fachtna turned to face the clashing, churning lake, raised her arms and called out in a strange language. Far out in the depths of the lake something disturbed the ice. Chunks shot into the air before plummeting back into the frigid waters. A wave rose and gathered strength as it pushed toward the shore, shoving ice floes aside as it came. It grew and grew until, a few metres from the shallows, it erupted in a volcanic spray and from its shattering green heart leaped two blue horses.

They galloped to the shore on stilt-like legs, sparks flying where their hoofs struck the wet stones. They circled Maddy, Danny and Roisin and paced with pent-up excitement. Their manes and tails were matted weeds, water streamed from their coats and they sniggered with human voices, their lips twisted into sneers that showed sharp canines. One pranced close to Maddy, its dark blue hide almost brushing her face. She gagged at the foul smell of water rot.

'These water horses will guard the shore,' said Fachtna. 'You must play the game alone and come to the Winter Court by no other route.'

'We can't cross that lake,' said Maddy. 'Look at it!'

'I've always heard such good things about mortal ingenuity,' said Fachtna, with just a touch of sarcasm in her voice. 'I'm sure you will find a way. Can't you swim?'

'We can swim,' said Danny, his voice almost as harsh as Fachtna's. 'But I don't think I'm going to make it through crashing sheets of ice and water that's below freezing.'

Fachtna cocked her head at him. 'Well, think of something, boy, and think of it quick. It would be an inglorious end to your quest were you to starve to death on this beach.'

With that, she spread her wings wide and took off into the moonlight, heading toward the tower.

CHAPTER NINETEEN

As soon as Fachtna disappeared from sight, the water horses stopped their prancing and began to sidle closer to the children. Maddy felt her trainers slither and slide on the ice-covered rocks as she backed toward the water's edge, George at her feet with his hackles raised. Roisin squealed with fear and ran down to the icy waves, but Danny bent and picked up a flat wide stone and hefted it in his palm.

'Another step,' he said, 'and one of you is going to get it right between the eyes.'

The horses paused for a moment, looked at each other and grinned.

'Such an unfriendly boy,' crooned one as it sidled ever closer. 'That's no way to treat a friend.'

'You're no friend of mine,' said Danny.

'Ah, but we could be, we could be,' said the other. 'If you treat us nicely, we could help you.'

'How?' said Maddy.

'Sit on our backs,' said the first. 'We can take you to the tower. The cold won't gnaw at you, not on our backs.'

'Why would you want to help us?' said Danny. 'Everyone who has helped us so far is going to die.'

'Liadan likes us,' said the first horse, running a black tongue over its lips. 'She wouldn't stay angry at us for long. And we like to be ridden. It's been a long, long time since anyone went with us into the waves.'

Something about the way the horse said that made Maddy shiver. The second one came closer to her and looked into her face. Its eyes were an utter, light-swallowing black. They radiated emptiness, a cold, deep dark vaster than space. *To fall into them*, said a voice in her mind, *would mean peace and untroubled, eternal sleep* . . .

'Will it hurt?' Maddy heard herself asking, her voice low and muffled in a suddenly silent world.

'No, child,' said the horse. 'It will be as easy as falling asleep.'

'I'm ready,' she whispered, reaching out a hand. The water horse sidled closer, rubbing its slimy mane against her open palm. Part of her brain registered how cold, how wet, how *dead* the flesh of the water horse felt, as it got to its knees and allowed her to slide a leg over its back until she was sitting astride. But she felt no revulsion, no desire to cringe away from its touch. She felt calm, as if she was floating. *It all feels so right*, she thought, as the weeds of the horse's mane waved in the air and wrapped themselves tight around her fingers and wrists. *This is the only way.*

Dimly she was aware of Danny and Roisin running alongside her as the horse began to trot to the water's edge, George barking furiously somewhere.

'Maddy, what are you saying? Get down!' cried Roisin, as she desperately pulled at Maddy's clothes.

'I said, "It can't hurt,"' said Maddy as the horse began to canter.

'No!' screamed Roisin. 'That's not what you said! Please, Maddy . . .' Her voice broke into a sob as the horse began to leave her and Danny behind and canter into the icy waters, its mate following close behind. 'Get down from its back! GET DOWN FROM ITS BACK!'

'It will be fine, Ro,' murmured Maddy, clinging tighter to the water horse's back with her thighs and knees as Danny and Roisin tried to grab her. Spray splashed her face as the animal galloped through the shallows, out into the heart of the lake. The water rose higher and soaked her jeans, then her jacket. Part of her noticed that the water was bitterly cold, but she felt disconnected from her body. The horse turned to look at her, an evil glint in its eye, and smiled, showing the cool curve of its fangs. She smiled back as Danny and Roisin's shouts were left behind her and the water horse plunged beneath the waves, the water snapping closed over her head, cutting off all sounds from the shore.

It was peaceful in the lake. *I can rest*, thought Maddy. *I just need to rest. It's all too hard.* The water horse curved its neck and took her deeper, its mate swimming alongside them, its back legs transformed into a long fish-scaled tail. *Much better*, thought Maddy. *Can't go swimming about with four legs.*

She looked up at the surface, so far above her head. The horse's muscles rippled beneath her, its mane streaming back into her face as the world got darker. Her chest was hurting now, real pain that was eclipsing the talon marks on her back. *I'll have to breathe out*, she thought dreamily.

She pondered the problem for a moment as the pain built and stars bloomed in the corners of her eyes. And then something bit her leg.

Maddy panicked and cried out, watching the last of her breath escape to the surface in mercury bubbles. The lake poured into her mouth and her hair floated around her face, blinding her. She thrashed about as the water horse bucked beneath her, her hands caught fast in its weedy mane.

The water boiled around her as dark shapes scudded through the gloom. For the first time since getting on the horse's back Maddy felt real terror, and it woke her up in a way the icy water had not. She could not see the surface any more, and however much she pulled and pulled, she couldn't free her hands. She opened her mouth to scream and more water poured into her lungs. Her vision turned dark as huge black shapes writhed through a mass of bubbles, tormenting the horse, which snapped and lunged in every direction. Just as she thought she was going to black out, Maddy felt a tugging at her wrists and then strong arms about her as she shot to the surface.

Her head broke through and she drew in a ragged breath, crystal clear air flooding her chest painfully. The night sky spun around her head as she coughed and spluttered, throwing up lake water as her rescuer sliced easily toward the shore with one arm.

Her feet scraped shingle and she staggered on rubbery legs, stumbling through the waves and ice to collapse on the rocks. She gasped as a huge shape loomed over, blotting out the sky.

'Stupid child!' it hissed. 'Next time you want to die, don't do it in our waters.'

Maddy sat up and stared as the shape turned away and called a wordless cry across the lake. It was a man, tall and broad-shouldered. He had long hair that hung in tangles around his face and shoulders, wore a fur cloak, and lake water ran off him in rivulets. He stared out across the water and Maddy followed his gaze. There, on an ice floe, were Roisin and Danny, George tucked away in Roisin's jacket, just his little head sticking out under her chin. George's eyes stood out on stalks as he stared at what was pushing them. Seals, dozens of them, were nudging the floe forward with their blunt heads, pushing it toward the shore.

As soon as they reached the shore, the man turned to look at her again and Maddy cringed, even as her body shook with cold. The face was hard and wild – there seemed to be no human emotion in it. His eyes were huge and velvety brown and his teeth were sharp and hard against his lips. He turned away from her and ran to the water, falling to his knees and wrapping the fur cloak tightly around himself. Then he seemed to roll into the water and disappear beneath it. She stared and stared, waiting to see his head break the surface, but when it did, it was a seal's sleek, whiskered face that appeared among the bobbing ice. It dived and its broad tail slapped the water as it dropped from sight. She held her breath to see the strange seal man again, but the surface of the lake was as empty as the moon.

'Who was that?' she croaked as Danny and Roisin scrambled up the beach toward her. They fell to their knees and hugged her, Roisin crying on her shoulder. 'What's going on?'

'Selkies, seal people,' said Danny. 'Almost as soon as you went under, they appeared in the water and asked us what happened. When we told them what you said, and that we were trying to get to the White Tower, they offered to help.'

'I thought no one could help us,' said Maddy through chattering teeth.

'That's the thing,' said Danny, grinning. 'Letting Fionn help us means the contract's broken so anyone can offer to help, and I don't think the selkies like Liadan much. We didn't swear another oath.' His face darkened. 'Of course, that can work against us as well, I think. It's a bit confusing.'

'Never mind that, what did you think you were *doing*?' snapped Roisin at Maddy.

'What?' asked Maddy, puzzled.

'Those water horses, they are dark faeries,' said Roisin. 'They tempt people on to their backs to drown them. The selkies said that only people who want to die get on the back of a water horse,' said Roisin. 'You were trying to kill yourself. Why would you do that?' Her eyes filled with tears again.

'I didn't!' said Maddy. 'I was just looking for a way to get across.'

'We heard you,' said Danny, his face set and angry. 'You asked that thing if it would hurt.'

'Did I?' said Maddy, searching her memories. 'I . . . I . . . don't remember.' She looked back at Danny and Roisin's frightened faces. 'I really don't!' George wriggled his front legs free of Roisin's grip and leaned forward to lick Maddy's icy skin. His warm, rough tongue practically burned her, she was so cold.

'Is that what you want?' asked Danny, his voice harsh. 'Is that what you're thinking about all the time at home? Is that why you act like you want everyone to hate you?'

Stunned, Maddy could only stare back at him. 'I don't think that way,' she said as her body started to shiver with the cold and her teeth chattered so hard she had to force each word out. 'I don't act like that.'

'Whatever, we've got to keep you moving,' said Roisin, as they pulled Maddy to her feet. She juddered and shuddered and her clothes clung to her.

'Where are we?' she asked.

'Turn round,' said Danny.

The lumpen caves were dark as midnight beneath the frilly fantasy of the upper reaches of the tower. There were no steps or doors carved anywhere into the white rock. They had reached Liadan's den.

'How are we supposed to get in?' asked Danny.

'Do you think we can go through the caves?' suggested Roisin, but her eyes were fearful.

'I don't fancy just walking in there,' said Maddy. 'Let's take a look around before we do anything.'

'We need to get you warm somehow,' said Roisin.

'Let's just walk for a few minutes – that will warm me up and we'll see what we can find out,' said Maddy.

chapter twenty

The twisting tower leaned over them, staggering against the moon. It blocked what little comfort there was from the silver rays, and the damp from the stones crept into their bones. A band of moonlight lit up a slice of shore that ran to meet the waves, but none of them suggested moving from under the oppressive shadow of the tower to walk by the whispering water. After everything they had seen today, Maddy didn't trust the lake any more. Who knew what was lurking beneath its surface?

They had not gone far when they heard the stamp and snort of horses from behind a pile of rocks that rose from the sand like the spine of a long-dead leviathan. Maddy froze, her eyes widening with fear. Were there more water horses waiting for her on the beach? She grabbed Roisin's hand in terror. Roisin looked at her, the same fear in her eyes, and held a finger to her lips.

'Tack,' she whispered. 'I can hear tack.'

Maddy clenched her chattering teeth and listened hard. Sure enough, there was the clink and jingle of buckled leather as horses shifted their weight on the pebbles. Whatever horses these were, someone had managed to saddle and bridle them.

They all looked at each other as the same thought flashed across their mind. Elven mounts!

Danny stooped and swept George up into his arms, clamping a hand firmly down on the little terrier's muzzle. Slowly they all crept toward the rocks, their bodies bent double, and peeped over the edge to the beach beyond.

There, standing out as sharp and vivid as an ink stain, was a team of six enormous black horses harnessed to a silent black coach. Its wheels were rimmed in silver that flashed and winked in the moonlight, while its wooden body was polished to such a shine that Maddy could see her face in its sides as clearly as in a mirror. The coachman seemed to be asleep. His body was bent over in the driving seat, swathed in a heavy black cloak, his head lost to view, no doubt hidden by the high stiff black collar. The horses were restless, and every time they snorted sparks and little jets of flame flew from their nostrils. Where they pawed the ground the earth was left blackened and steaming.

'Do you think it's waiting for us?' asked Roisin, her whisper hoarse in the silence.

At the sound of her voice the coachman's body stiffened and he turned in his seat to look at them. But where his head should have been, there was nothing. There was a rustle and looking down they saw the coachman's hands turning his head in his lap.

A hideous, idiotic grin split the pale face from ear to ear, and the small black eyes darted about like malignant flies. The head didn't seem to have noticed them, but the body leaned toward them with dreadful intent. It raised its arm and with stiffened black-gloved fingers tapped the side of the coach, twice, before pointing to the door. It then stayed absolutely motionless, still pointing at the door, as if frozen in time.

'Anyone heard any stories about this guy?' Danny asked. Maddy and Roisin shook their heads, panting with fear.

'I think he wants us to get in the coach,' said Maddy, terror making her squeak. Her body had forgotten even to shiver.

'No way!' said Danny, his eyes wide. 'Unless we know and like how his story ends, I'm not going anywhere in that thing.'

'He's not making a move toward us though,' said

Maddy. 'I think Liadan may have sent him. He's waiting for us.'

Roisin let go of Danny and stood looking at the coach, her hands clenching and unclenching by her sides. Maddy heard her mutter, 'Right!' under her breath, before she marched across the rocky beach to the coach and climbed in, leaving the door open behind her. The gloom inside the black coach swallowed her whole.

Maddy and Danny looked at each other and then at the coach. Maddy felt the tension build up in her chest as she realized she had stopped breathing and forced herself to take a deep breath, waiting for something to happen. But the coachman sat there, still pointing at the door.

'I think he wants us all in there,' Danny said.

Roisin's face reappeared from the gloom. 'Are the two of you getting in or what?' she demanded. 'I don't think he's leaving without you.'

'Roisin, what are you doing?' said Danny in a strangled voice.

She frowned at him. 'Liadan isn't going to try to kill us until *after* we get to the tower, so I reckon we're safer with this guy than with anything else that might be wandering around out here,' she said, before pulling her head back in. Her words sounded brave, but her face was white.

Danny looked at Maddy in shock. Maddy shrugged just as Roisin yelled, 'Come on, let's get on with it!'

Stung into action, Maddy and Danny half ran to the coach. Danny stepped up to the door, but as Maddy pushed a reluctant George into the boxy interior, she paused to look up at the coachman, who up close seemed to be as enormous as his horses. His body and clothes were an indistinguishable black, but his pale, bald head glowed with a sickly green light. His eyes never stopped darting in their sockets. It was as if the head and body had nothing to do with each other. The smell of musty clothes and decay washed over her and she suppressed a shudder as she put her foot on the carriage step and vaulted inside.

As soon as she was in the coach, the door was slammed shut by an invisible hand and she was thrown back against the black velvet seat as the horses lurched forward into a gallop. She would have screamed with fear had she been able to take a breath, but the coach bowled along the shore with unnatural speed. They were all thrust back against the seat, and as the coach rattled along, Maddy felt her internal organs sloshing around inside her, bruising against her ribcage. *Now I know why Hobbs called me a meat bag*, she thought.

It didn't seem possible, but the coach was gaining speed. Maddy could see that Danny and Roisin were pinned to the seat with their elbows and necks at odd angles, the flesh juddering on their faces. George rolled back against the foot of the coach seat, paws splayed on the floor and his lips peeling back from his teeth from the g-force. The wind screamed as the coach sliced through it.

With every muscle straining in her arms, Maddy let go of George's lead and pushed against Danny to propel herself to the window in the door. Pressing her face to the glass she could see sparks flying off the wheels. The scenery outside blurred past but she could see that they were climbing higher and higher, hugging a road along the tower walls as they rose. The hoofs of the horses thundered through the yowling wind, but from the coachman there was not a single sound.

Soon they stormed through a gateway in the tower. Massive, ornate copper gates reared up in their path, and just as it seemed the coach would crash into them, they flew open. On and on they raced, higher and higher, images of ruined houses and crumbling streets flashing past the window.

Suddenly the coach stopped, throwing the three children to the floor. George yowled and scrabbled out from under their groaning bodies. With shaking fingers Maddy pawed at the door handle and the four of them tumbled out on to stone steps, staggering from side to side as they tried to recover. Maddy felt as if every bone in her body had been shaken to powder, leaving her with floppy arms and legs.

She straightened up and tried to still her swimming vision. Dimly she heard the coach rumble away at a more sedate pace. As her surroundings sharpened into focus she became aware of a white-clad figure picking its way down some stone steps in front of her. The steps rose to a hall fronted by fluting columns that flanked vast wooden double doors black with age.

As Maddy looked around, she could see that they were standing in a courtyard of broken flagstones. All around them the inner walls of the tower twisted upwards, folding like petals around the hall at its centre and turning in until the distant sky was a small O far above. Beams of moonlight criss-crossed the tower's interior, tumbling and bouncing off polished discs set into the crumbling walls before breaking against the hall. The hall itself was as neat and simple as the shabby and decayed tower was overblown and fanciful. It was as if a sophisticated marble temple had been set down inside a castle created by a child. Frost and snow lay over all the flaws and smoothed them to the eye, but Maddy could see that the tower was sick. She guessed that Liadan had created it to swallow the hall, which must have been the home of the Tuatha who had ruled before her. *Look at me!* the tower seemed to say. *Look at how grand and tall and impressive I am compared to what the old queen built. Is the new queen not wonderful?*

Nutter, thought Maddy.

The tip-tapping of a woman's shoes on the stairs brought Maddy back to the present. She was beautiful and dressed in white furs over a flowing white dress that dragged in a train behind her. Jewels dripped from her ears and neck and crusted her elegant, tapering fingers. Her dress was embroidered all over with plants, birds and butterflies, making her a promise of Spring in Winter's home. Her hair was blonde and hung in huge glossy waves to her knees. A smile hovered on her lips and her green eyes were full of laughter. But her white hands were forced to hold up the edges of her dress as she carefully made her way toward them, and it wasn't high heels that made her feet ring against the stone. She had no feet, only the cloven hoofs and thick hairy legs of a goat.

With her teeth still vibrating in her head from the coach ride, Maddy could only gawp at the faerie. When she was a couple of steps from the children, the creature stopped and dipped in a slight bow.

'Lady Aoife, at your service,' she said. 'My mistress, Queen Liadan, bids you welcome to the Winter Court.'

CHApTER TWENTY-ONE

Maddy looked up at the woman and tried to get her jellied tongue to work.

Aoife laughed, a bright, tinkling sound that cascaded through the frigid air. 'Compose yourself, honoured guest,' she said. 'A ride with the dullahan can be quite breathtaking.'

'Bring Stephen out,' said Maddy, when the muscles in her mouth had solidified. 'We have kept to our side of the bargain, so bring Stephen out here now.'

Aoife smiled. 'You have kept your side of the bargain?' she echoed. 'I think not. You've had a lot of help getting here. And still you were so slow, My Lady felt compelled to have the dullahan deliver you.' She frowned, anger clouding her bright face. 'You have been untruthful from the start, so do not make demands on this court with your vulgar speech. Faeries, unlike humans, cannot lie. You will have your lost child soon. But first you will attend an audience with Queen Liadan.'

Maddy ground her teeth in frustration. 'Fine.' She bit the word out. 'Let's get this over with.'

They all started to follow Lady Aoife toward the steps, but the faerie held up a hand to stop Danny and Roisin. 'Queen Liadan requests only you come before her,' she said to Maddy. 'She finds it exhausting conversing with mortals and does not wish to deal with more than one of you at a time.'

'Why?' asked Roisin.

'Your minds work in a very different way to the minds of faeries and your deceitful natures can be quite . . . wearing,' said Aoife.

'Charming,' muttered Danny.

Maddy looked Aoife in the eye. 'I'm not going in there on my own.'

Anger flashed again in Aoife's eyes. 'Do not insult us!' she snapped. 'You have the word of the Winter Queen herself that you will not be harmed until the hunt starts.'

Maddy turned to look at Danny and Roisin. Danny put his arm around his trembling sister, who looked up at Maddy and shrugged before sinking down at the bottom of the stone steps, huddling against their edges.

'What's the point in arguing?' she said. 'They're not going to kill us yet, at any rate. They want their hunt.'

'You go on in. We'll be waiting for you when you come out. Promise,' said Danny, before sitting down behind Roisin and lacing his fingers through hers. Roisin closed her eyes as tears spilled down her cheeks.

Maddy looked at their bowed heads and swallowed a lump in her throat. Sitting so close together it struck her how alike they were in their gestures and features. They were family; they had what she had lost. Her eyes burned with hot tears, but then Danny looked up at her. 'We're not leaving without you, Maddy. And if you're not out soon, we're coming in to get you.'

Maddy wanted to sit down and put her arms around them both, go to sleep and pretend this place didn't exist. Instead she merely nodded at Danny, turned her back and began to climb the steps toward Aoife. The faerie's face shone bright with pleasure again and she turned and led the way to the doors.

There was a clicking noise on the steps behind them, and Maddy turned to see George trotting after her, a determined look on his face. Aoife raised an eyebrow and opened her mouth to say something, but Maddy cut her off.

'Forget it,' she snapped. 'You can't say anything about him – he can't talk, much less lie.'

Aoife frowned and then nodded. 'Very well. But if you value him, keep him close. Oh, and one more thing.' The faerie laid a hand on Maddy's soaking-wet arm, sending a pulse of warmth through her. Her skin warmed and steam rose from her clothes.

'A gift, to make you comfortable,' said Lady Aoife. She wrinkled her pretty nose. 'A pity I can do nothing about the smell.'

The huge doors were standing slightly ajar, just enough for Aoife to slip through. Maddy followed her and the doors boomed shut behind her, locks and bolts clicking and whirring and sliding into place. George jumped at the noise and pressed himself against her leg.

When her eyes adjusted she found herself standing in a hall dominated by high arched windows that flooded the room with cold moonlight, filtered down from above, caught and magnified and thrown about the room by more giant silver mirrors that were propped up on ornately carved stone easels. Fluted columns carved with twisting vines and flowers rose up to support a roof decorated with hunting scenes, and everything gleamed in rich jewel colours. The moonlight lit the hall up as bright as day, but warm yellow candles burned brightly where the deepest shadows lay. Outside might be virginal and plain beneath the snow and ice, but in here was decadence and wealth and beauty. Even the cold air was perfumed, and thick carpets muffled noise beneath the columns as effectively as snow.

At the far end of the room, a crystal throne stood between two windows, shafts of reflected moonlight shattering against it to set its edges twinkling. Aoife was walking toward the throne to bend and whisper in the ear of the woman seated there. Queen Liadan.

Her hair was a black river that flowed over her simple ivory dress to puddle at her tiny feet. Her skin was as smooth and white as fresh snow and her cheeks and lips were stained as red as blood. *Snow White*, thought Maddy. *I'm looking at Snow White.* Around her stood her court, luminous elves dressed as rich as she was plain, in embroidered silks and elaborate brocades, heavy furs draped across their shoulders and fastened with silver and gold brooches. Their eyes and even their fingernails glittered like diamonds in the light as they clapped their jewelled fingers. Their mocking laughter was as light and sweet as breaking glass.

Maddy felt small and dirty and ugly as she began her lonely walk on uncarpeted flagstones that marked a path to the foot of the throne. Her fingers itched to comb her tangled brown hair. Aoife had been right: Maddy stank, and her face and hands were streaked with dirt. Blood still crusted her nose from when she had fallen on the ice, and the sour taste of bile coated her mouth. Her now dry T-shirt stuck to the dried blood on the wounds on her back and the fabric pulled at her every now and then. George sauntered beside her, his chest puffed out in a show of bravado, smelling to high heaven of wet, dirty fur.

Aoife stepped down from the dais of the throne and went to sit on its left with a group of women who all had cloven hoofs peeping from under their lovely gowns. While the elves shone cruel and bright, there were other, darker, more unwholesome forms gathering among the pillars. Green-skinned pixies stood knee high to lumpen, glowering trolls whose tusks curved up from their lower jaws. Banshees clawed at their hair, plucked at their grey rags, and watched Maddy with eyes that burned like coals. Red-skinned men covered in thorns grinned at her menacingly from the shadows. Smaller twisted shapes scampered between the legs of these horrors, like children at a carnival. Maddy clenched her fists as the familiar leering face of Sean Rua winked at her from beneath his mop of red hair, before he dived behind the legs of a glowering knight dressed in black armour. She took a deep breath and reminded herself there was no time to go after Sean Rua now. She would get Stephen back, and if she survived this, she was going to punch the living daylights out of that child-stealing faerie if he ever set foot in Blarney again.

She had almost reached the foot of the throne when a movement to her left caught her eye. There, gleaming bone white in the shadows between the mirrors, was Fachtna. The dark faerie sat sprawled in a carved wooden chair, her pointed chin resting in the palm of her hand as she watched Maddy. Her face was smooth and blank. Her other hand gripped heavy silver chains, which were attached to the collars of the most gruesome creatures there. They looked like dogs as they strained against their leashes and snapped their huge jaws at her, but their bodies were a boiling mass of darkness. Maddy blinked and tried to see them properly, but they blurred and shifted so she only caught glimpses of scales, claws, folded leathery wings and fur. Scucca hounds, she realized. She cried out in fear and flinched away when one massive beast lunged at her, causing the whole court to erupt into laughter. George snarled back, but she gripped his collar tight. The fir dorocha stood behind Fachtna's chair, their bodies shadowy and indistinct. The only thing that stood out was their eyes, pinpricks of light that gleamed in their formless faces. Fear wafted from them like cheap aftershave.

Maddy swallowed and walked on, stopping a few metres from the foot of the throne. Her back felt cold and vulnerable and her fingers curled into her palms, longing for a warm hand to hold. George pressed his muscly little body against her leg. She looked up at Liadan and just as quickly dropped her eyes.

Fionn had said that the Winter crown had cost Liadan dear. Now Maddy could see how enormous that price had been.

Up close, Liadan was a ruined beauty. The colour in her cheeks and lips had been painted on. Her eyes were white with just the faintest smudge of a pupil, all colour boiled away by the ferocious cold. Her long fingers were curled into claws, the joints and knuckles painfully swollen. Cold radiated out from her bare feet, the frost creeping across the flagstones to Maddy's trainers. What must once have been unearthly beauty haunted her in her glossy hair, her slight frame and the curve of her cheek. Now her body was twisted with pain and the cold burned in her, lighting her up with its hunger. When she spoke, her voice was the relentless grind of a glacier as it crushed and ground everything beneath its bulk.

'Tedious child, you stand before me at last,' said Liadan. 'I thought you would never arrive.'

'I am here now and ready to honour our bargain,' said Maddy. 'Give me Stephen and then I will do as you ask and run from your hunt.'

'Ah, yes,' Liadan's voice groaned from her brittle chest. 'The little child who has caused all this trouble.

Tell me, now that you have seen this land, do you still wish to try to return home?'

'Of course,' said Maddy.

'What say you?' she called to her court. 'Here comes this little mortal, fashioning herself as a hero. She dares to defy us. Shall we see if we can make her betray her quest?'

As the court roared its approval, Maddy felt her heart sink. Liadan was going to make this as hard as possible.

'Hmmm, how shall we test you?' asked the Winter Queen, as she sat back in her throne and drummed her twisted fingers on its arm. 'Are you too young for a kiss from a gancanagh? Connor, show yourself.'

A dark-haired man stepped from the crowds that lurked beneath the pillars and bowed to Maddy, giving her a warm smile. He was so beautiful it made her throat ache to look at him. But she shook her head and tore her gaze away from him to look at Liadan.

'Please, give me Stephen,' she said.

'Alas, Connor, the child is impervious to your charms – the first mortal to be so in a long time,' Liadan commented. The hall erupted into laughter and the dark-haired faerie smiled and stepped back into the crowd.

'If you are too young for a kiss, perhaps a mother is what you crave,' said Liadan, waving one hand at the goat-legged women. 'One of my glaistigs would no doubt love to take the post. They may look strange to your eyes, but they are very maternal.'

The glaistigs giggled and blew Maddy kisses while the Winter Court's laughter turned shrill and mocking.

'I have a mother, Majesty, and I have no wish to replace her,' said Maddy. 'Please, if you will, give me Stephen as you promised.'

'You have no mother, for she is dead,' said Liadan. 'What use is a dead mother?'

'She is more than enough for me,' said Maddy, her voice low as anger began to boil.

'Does she rock you to sleep? Comfort you when you are sick?' asked Liadan.

'No.'

'Then I ask again, what use is a dead mother?'

Maddy ground her teeth. 'I couldn't tell you, Majesty, but to me, she is enough.'

'How pathetic. Is that really the best answer you can give?' asked Liadan, her painted mouth twisting in an ugly sneer, a vicious wound in the ravaged face. Maddy said nothing. 'Very well,' she sighed. 'Bring the child forth.'

A ripple went through the group of glaistigs and they parted to show a dark-haired one among them sitting with Stephen curled up asleep in her lap. She gathered the slumbering child in her arms and stepped toward

Maddy, her hoofs trip-trapping over the flagstones. Maddy snatched him from the faerie and snuggled him close, kissing his hair and breathing in the warm, soft, familiar smell of him. She bit back a sob of relief when she saw the plastic dinosaur still clutched in his chubby fist. Stephen lay limp in her arms, his eyes roving restlessly beneath blue-veined lids, a frown puckering his face. She wrapped his dressing gown tighter around him and put her lips to his ear.

'Stephen, wake up, darling,' she said. 'It's Maddy, I've come to take you home. Stephen?' But Stephen slept on.

She looked up at Liadan.

'He is unharmed, as you promised?' she asked.

'Not one hair on his head has been hurt,' said Liadan. 'My ladies-in-waiting have cared for him as if he was their own.'

'So why isn't he awake?' asked Maddy.

'A harmless glamour to save him distress,' said Liadan airily. 'My soft-hearted attendants could not bear to see him cry. He will wake as soon as he gets home.'

'So that's it?' asked Maddy. 'We can go now? No more trying to tempt me to stay?'

'No, I think a night's hunting will be much more fun,' said Liadan, yawning. 'You are free to run.'

'How am I supposed to get off this island?' Maddy asked.

'That's not really my concern, nor is it part of our bargain,' said Liadan.

'No, but it will be a short and boring hunt if we just run round and round the tower,' said Maddy. 'It would benefit you to help us off the island and give us a head start.'

Again laughter roared up to the painted roof.

Liadan smiled, a cold, ghastly imitation of the real thing. 'Let us hope you can run as fast as you talk, little one,' she said.

She stood and made her painful way down the dais to Maddy. One shoulder hunched and a foot dragged behind ever so slightly, giving her a shuffling step. Maddy involuntarily jerked away from the cold that splashed around the queen as she walked past her toward the double doors at the back of the hall. Maddy fell in behind her, as did the rest of the court. She noticed that all of them took great care to keep their feet beyond the frost that shivered from Liadan's every step.

The golden bolts and locks on the doors began to whirr and click into life as Liadan approached, shooting bolts and turning tumblers as her bone-numbing cold reached out and patterned their lower reaches with ice. She held out her arms and cried out and the doors flew open at her approach. At the foot of the steps, Danny and Roisin stood and gazed open-mouthed as Liadan picked her way toward them, Maddy, Stephen, George and her court trailing in her wake.

'Ah yes, the spares,' said Liadan as she caught sight of them. 'Come with us.'

Warily, Danny and Roisin fell into step next to Maddy.

Roisin frowned when she saw Stephen in such a deep sleep in Maddy's arms. 'Why doesn't he wake up?' she asked.

'He will,' said Maddy grimly, hugging the little boy closer to her. 'He will. We just have to get him home.'

Liadan made her painful, crippled way down the road that led to the lakeside. After the long descent to the shore, she walked to the edge of the waves, crouched and put a hand in the water.

As soon as her skin touched the waves, the surface of the lake shuddered like an animal. Water began to turn to ice around her wrist and she called out a single word. The ice floes collided and crushed themselves to fine power against each other. The powder mingled with the stiffening waves until, in a matter of seconds, an ice bridge stretched from shore to shore.

'Cross quickly while the bridge holds,' said Liadan. 'Once your feet touch the soil on the other side, the hunt starts. You will be shown no mercy.'

Maddy nodded and turned to go.

'One more thing,' said Liadan, and Maddy turned back to face her, Stephen cradled against her chest. 'If it's to be a proper hunt, then the hounds should follow a blood trail. Don't you think?'

Maddy looked at her in confusion. Before she had time to react, Liadan closed the gap between them and grabbed Maddy's shoulder. Shards of ice shot from her fingertips and slid straight through Maddy's skin.

Maddy's heart missed a beat and all the sound in the world rushed out of her ears. She clutched Stephen even tighter and stared stupidly at the white fingers hooked into her skin and the hot red blood that pattered on to Stephen's fine blond hair. Somewhere she could hear Roisin and Danny shouting. When Liadan let go, Maddy sank to her knees, her legs too weak from shock to hold her up. Sound rushed back in a wave and broke over her head.

'What are you doing?' yelled Roisin, restraining a barking George from biting Liadan, as Danny ran to Maddy's side. 'You promised you wouldn't hurt us!'

'Only on the journey toward me,' hissed Liadan, her boiled eyes narrowed to slits. 'I made no such provision for the journey away.'

With that she turned on her heel and swept back toward the tower, her court still following in her wake.

'Come on, Maddy, we've got to get out of here,' said

Danny, hooking his arms underneath her armpits and hauling her to her feet. Maddy yelled with pain as he lifted her, her body jerking with the cold that spread from her shoulder like an infection. Her breath came in shallow gulps, but her head was drenched in hot sweat. Roisin rushed to take Stephen from her, while Danny pulled one of her arms around his neck and set off along the ice bridge, making her scream again as her wound was jolted.

She could barely keep her head up as the cold spread through her body. George raced across the bridge, urging them on with barks that were high and sharp with anxiety. Danny dragged Maddy, her feet tripping over each other as she sobbed, her breath hitching in her chest.

'Keep going,' he grunted. 'We're nearly there. Just a little bit further.'

After what seemed like an eternity they half fell, half slid from the bridge on to the far shore. Maddy collapsed on to the ground and curled up, giving in to the pain. Across the lake she could hear the mournful cry of a hunting horn. The Winter Court's hunt was riding out, and she couldn't take another step.

CHAPTER TWENTY-TWO

Danny leaned over her. 'Maddy, you have to get up! We have to run!'

She shook her head at him. 'I . . . can't,' she gasped.

'Please, Maddy,' Danny begged. 'The forest is just a few metres behind you. If we can get deep enough inside it, we can hide or find help. You can't give up now!'

Maddy groaned and shook her head. Roisin knelt on the ground and rocked Stephen to and fro, her face buried in his blood-matted hair.

'Maddy, if you don't run, they are going to get us, and everything we've been through won't matter,' said Danny. 'They'll kill us all – you know they will. Please get up!'

'Leave me,' said Maddy. 'Take Stephen and get out of here. Run for the mound.'

'I'm not doing that,' said Danny, his teeth clenched.

'You have to,' said Maddy. 'I'm sorry. I never thought

things would get so serious.' George whimpered and nuzzled her cheek with his cold nose.

Behind them, the tower burst into activity. Lights blazed in every window, while shouts of excitement and high-pitched whinnies drifted across the lake.

Danny looked at Roisin. 'You can get us out of here, Ro.'

She raised a tear-streaked face. 'Me? I can't do anything,' she said.

'Yes, you can,' said Danny. 'We need to be clever to get out of this, and you're the smart one. Think, Ro! What do we need to get us out of here?'

George began to growl and Maddy turned her head to look back at the tower. Pennants were fluttering and white mounts were racing along the winding road that led from the tower down to the beach. Brightly dressed faeries sat astride them, and the shadowy fir dorocha were out in front, whipping on the baying scucca hounds.

'Better make it fast, Ro.' Maddy coughed with the effort it took to speak. She closed her eyes as the cold bit at muscle and nerve.

George wedged his body between her neck and shoulder and began to lick her face frantically with his hot tongue.

Roisin's head snapped up and she stared at them. 'That's it!' she cried.

'What?' said Danny. 'Have you thought of something?'

'We can't outsmart them or make them leave us alone, so we need to outrun them,' said Roisin. 'We need something very fast and something that can carry us between the two worlds.'

'It would need to be very, very quick,' said Maddy. The hunt had reached the bridge now and was beginning to pour across it. The baying of the hounds was sharp and sounded all too close. The ice bridge boomed as the mounts began to thunder across, Fachtna's in the lead.

'Well, like what?' said Danny. 'Quick, Ro!'

'Shut up, I'm thinking!' she snapped. She bent her head and closed her eyes. 'This world is a dream, right? Nothing here would exist if the Morrighan didn't dream it.'

'That's what Fionn said,' said Danny. 'What of it?'

'Think about it,' said Roisin. 'If it's a dream, then we can influence it, right? We can dream inside the dream and it will happen.'

'I have no idea what you're talking about,' said Danny.

'What's the effect Hobbs said we have on this place?' said Roisin. 'We pollute it.' She raised a finger and tapped the side of her head. 'We pollute it with what we've got up here.' She turned to look at the hunt as it charged across the bridge. It was now halfway across and Maddy could see tongues of flame belching from the hounds' mouths as they raced toward them, the whips of the fir dorocha curling over their heads, driving them on.

'We can give the Morrighan nightmares,' said Roisin thoughtfully, as the hunt raced closer.

'Roisin, my life is flashing in front of my eyes, never mind my dreams!' yelled Danny. 'If you've got a plan, go for it!'

Roisin smiled and scraped away some of the pebbles, placing her hands flat against the bare earth beneath.

'Those mounts are pretty scary,' she grinned. 'Let's make some of our own.'

For a moment nothing happened, and then shadows that clung to the rocks and the trees and even huddled beneath the lip of the ice bridge began to run together, forming three distinct patches. The pools of shadow grew bigger and bigger. They swirled and became heavier and darker, until they lay solid as flesh on the ground. They were still for a moment and then they started to ripple and churn. In the writhing mass, clear shapes began to emerge. Horse heads stretched out into the clear air, followed by long muscular necks. Broad backs and flat flanks began to take form in front of Maddy's eyes, until the last of the shadows solidified into long, lean legs. The ground blazed white without its shadows, and three gigantic black horses looked down at the children as they huddled on the ground. The animals' edges blurred if you stared at them, and as they moved the sounds of crying and weeping wafted faintly about them.

'What are they?' asked Maddy.

'They're nightmares,' crowed Roisin. 'Geddit?'

'Pure genius, Ro,' yelled Danny. 'Pure, bloody genius!'

'Of course.' She grinned.

Danny helped Maddy to her feet. She swayed when she stood, numb to every thought and sensation other than the sickening pain that was spreading through her. *I'll never manage this*, she thought, as the baying of the hounds and the bloodthirsty cries of the Winter Court got closer and closer. Fionn's tear-stained face floated in front of her. *How stupid am I?*

George whimpered, holding one paw in the air as his eyes roved around her face. The mare closest to her seemed to hear Maddy's thoughts. She walked over and lay down. Maddy grabbed a handful of mane and scraped her leg over the mare's ribs. The nightmare climbed back to her feet, with Maddy lying along her back, her pale, sweating face laid against the long neck. As the cold tightened its grip on her chest, Maddy's breath was beginning to wheeze in and out of her lungs. George began to keen, rising up on his back legs to get closer to her. She reached out a hand to reassure him.

'Can you do this?' asked Danny.

She gave him a weak smile. 'I haven't got much choice.'

The other two mares offered their backs to Danny and Roisin. Danny grabbed George and zipped him tight into his jacket before climbing on board. Roisin swung a leg over with easy confidence, cradling Stephen with one arm. She grabbed a fistful of mane.

'Hold on tight,' she said, before flicking the horse's flanks with her heels and urging her on. The nightmare bunched her muscles and leaped forward, galloping away into the forest, her sisters racing to keep up with her. Behind them, the disappointed shrieks of the hunt rose in the air, scattering sleeping birds from the trees.

The nightmares moved through the Land of Eternal Youth like a haunting. The trees slid past them in silence. There was no drumming of hoofs, no impact with the ground to jolt Maddy's pain-racked body. Just the easy clench and release of muscle as the nightmare stretched out beneath her and the sound of breathing mingling with the quiet of the night forest. Maddy lay her cheek against the satin skin and closed her eyes as the faerie world rushed past.

Her eyes snapped open as the nightmare skidded to a halt. They had reached the mound, but there was no opening to be seen. It squatted in the night, a grass hillock, nothing more. It certainly offered no hope of escape.

'What do we do now?' asked Roisin. The nightmares had outrun the hunt, but it was catching up. Already the faint cries of the hounds and the excited shouts of the riders drifted toward them on the wind.

'I think we have to get out the same way we got in,' said Danny grimly, jumping off his nightmare and walking toward Maddy. She looked down at him. 'Sorry about this,' he said.

'What?' she asked.

'This,' said Danny, and he reached up and pressed his hand against the wound in her shoulder. Maddy yelped in pain and clutched at the nightmare's neck as she swayed with dizziness.

'What was that for?' she wheezed.

'I'm really, really sorry,' said Danny, looking sheepish as he walked toward the mound, holding his hand out before him. 'But you are the only one of us who is bleeding already, so it's just easier . . .' He leaned down and rubbed his bloody hand on the wet grass that blanketed the mound.

Maddy held her breath and waited. After what seemed like an eternity, the front of the mound fell away, soil and rock rumbling and pattering down the side of the hill. A square-cut tunnel led into the dark hill.

'Let's go,' said Roisin, kicking her heels against her nightmare's flanks while Danny scrambled to get back on his own horse.

The nightmares flowed through the ink-black tunnel, racing deep into the earth. There was a dull light up ahead, but when they raced out of the tunnel, instead of entering a domed room at the heart of the mound, they found themselves in the black sand desert.

There was nowhere to run to. There was no end to the desert. The sand stretched to the horizon.

'Where do we go from here?' said Danny. 'What do we do now? Are we supposed to just imagine our way back to Blarney?'

'I don't know,' said Roisin. 'I'm trying to imagine it, but nothing's happening.'

The sound of a hunting horn and a dreadful baying drifted over the sand – the scucca hounds were right behind them.

'They're catching up with us!' yelled Danny. George popped his head out of his jacket and started barking. 'They're coming through the mound!' The little terrier was yapping fit to burst.

'George, not now!' said Roisin. 'Shut up and give me a second to think.'

Maddy raised her head and looked at the dog. 'Look,' she croaked, pointing at him.

'What?' said Danny. 'I don't see anything.'

'Look what he's barking at,' said Maddy.

George was barking with a steady rhythm. His body was tense and quivering and his noise pointed up, straight at the weak sun that burned overhead. A sun that wasn't setting, unlike the sun in their world or the Land of Eternal Youth.

'We're in the mound,' said Maddy. 'He thinks we've gone to earth.'

'That's it!' said Roisin. 'He's a hunting dog. He thinks we're in a rabbit warren and he's pointing the way out.'

Danny looked up, his forehead creasing with doubt. 'The sun? He's pointing us at the sun?'

'Daylight,' said Roisin, 'at the end of the tunnel.'

'But how do we get there?' said Maddy.

Roisin looked up, tugged on her nightmare's mane, kicked her feet against her ribs and cried, 'Up!'

It was that simple. The nightmare reared and launched herself into the air, heading straight for the weak disc. Maddy flung her arms around her nightmare's neck as she felt the animal stand up on her back legs before leaping. She closed her eyes and heard Danny whoop with excitement behind her.

The wind whistled in Maddy's ears and prised at her eyelids. Then it was dark and she was being squashed and squeezed. She fought against the temptation to open her mouth and scream, convinced soil would flood into her chest rather than air. A roaring noise filled her ears and the mare exploded out of the mound in a shower of dirt, before landing gracefully.

Maddy opened her eyes and slid carefully off the mare's back. As soon as her feet touched the ground, the nightmare began to dissolve. Maddy stroked her soft nose as she faded away. 'Thank you,' she whispered. The horse rumbled in her throat and nuzzled Maddy's face before the shadows drifted apart.

'It's snowing here,' said Roisin. 'We've got to get off this mound!'

Maddy staggered and turned to look at the mouth of the tunnel yawning behind them. They were home, back in Blarney, and Stephen was safe. Surely Liadan and Fachtna would have turned the hunt back? There was a faint sound, a whisper of noise that curled up from the black mouth of the tunnel. Maddy strained her ears to listen. There it was, the faint but unmistakable sound of hounds giving tongue. The hunt was still coming.

Clutching Stephen to her, Roisin ran for the edge of the mound and the sheets of pouring rain that showed where the mortal world started and the faerie ended. George scrabbled free of Danny's jacket and pulled at the hem of Maddy's jeans, urging her on. Danny grabbed Maddy's arm and dragged her down the hill.

Thunder and lightning exploded around the mound, lighting up the castle grounds like the flash of a camera and blinding Maddy momentarily. She willed her legs to keep moving, but just when they were almost there she collided with something she couldn't see. Danny kept on running, losing his grip on her jacket as he ran off the hill. But Maddy was thrown back by the force of her collision, her teeth jarring in her head.

Stunned, she climbed to her feet and tried again. The same invisible barrier repelled her like a sheet of glass. Danny and Roisin had turned to see where she was and she could read the horror on their faces and their mouths moving as they called to her. George was barking and scrabbling at the barrier with his front paws. Stephen was waking in Roisin's arms, his face crumpling in distress. But she couldn't hear them. It was as if she was watching TV with the sound switched off.

But with awful clarity she could hear the hunt gaining on her. The cries of the hounds and the riders were clearer now as they drifted from the mouth of the tunnel behind. Another few seconds and they would be on her. She lifted her hand and hit out at the wall. It rippled from the force of her blow, but she still couldn't force her way through. Then a man appeared behind Danny and Roisin, walking in the rain with the collar of his coat turned up. He lifted his head to look at her, and

Maddy cried out in misery as she recognized Granda, gripping a spitting, struggling changeling firmly by the neck. She saw the fear in his eyes as she tried to reach for him but was again thrown back.

She began to cry, beating at the barrier with her fists. In front of her, Danny, Granda and Roisin ran their shoulders against the other side, but it was no use. Maddy was sealed in as tight as a figurine in a snow globe.

She slid to her knees. Hot tears carved tracks through the grime on her face. She put her hand against the skin that was stopping her from stepping across into safety, and Granda put his palm against hers.

'Why is this happening to me?' she wept. He shook his head. Then his eyes looked past her, widening in fear. She saw Danny and Roisin shouting and pointing.

She didn't need to turn her head to see what they meant. She could smell the elven mounts and hear the chink of their bridles. The scucca hounds growled and snapped and the Winter Court chattered and laughed, no doubt in high excitement at the thought of killing Maddy. There was a soft thud in the snow and then she heard that slow, dragging step.

She bent her head.

It was over.

CHAPTER TWENTY-THREE

'How did you ever think you could go home, child?' asked Liadan. Maddy didn't answer and turned her head away, refusing to lift her eyes to meet that dead white gaze. Liadan bent her head until her mouth was a few centimetres from Maddy's ear. Her breath froze the delicate hairs on Maddy's face, encasing them in tiny slivers of ice.

'The same rules apply going back as going out,' she said. 'If you cannot see it or believe it, then you can't step into it. For tonight, this is faerie soil, and home is a wish.'

She pointed at Danny and Roisin. 'Now, your companions there, they didn't have to think about it too hard,' she continued. 'They saw they were home, and they ran straight into it. The little one could do it even as he slept. But you?' Liadan sighed and crouched down next to Maddy, her ivory dress fanning out around her.

'Your people have a saying: "Home is where the heart is."
And your heart is gone.'

Anger flared in Maddy's chest. 'What do you mean?'
she asked.

'Your parents taught you that Ireland was home,
didn't they? But you don't feel at home here. And you
don't feel at home in that great grey city either, because
your parents didn't. So home was where your parents
were. And now they're dead, leaving you an unwanted,
unloved child, with no place to go in the world. You
would have been better off dead too.'

'So kill me then,' said Maddy bitterly. 'Isn't that what
you want?'

'Actually, no,' said Liadan. 'It was amusing to chase
you, but I have bigger plans for you.'

'So you lied,' said Maddy. 'You broke the rules.'

'No, I meant it when I said I wanted to hunt you, but
I didn't say I wanted to kill you, did I?' Liadan went on,
her head cocked to one side. '*You* are the one who broke
the rules. You made a bargain, and then you broke it.
Silly, silly girl.'

'So what do you want?' asked Maddy.

'Let me show you something,' said Liadan. She made
a gesture with one hand, and a moving image hung in
the air between herself and Maddy.

Maddy cried out in fear and scrambled back when

she looked at it and realized she was staring at a cloaked and hooded figure wielding a scythe.

Liadan laughed. 'How you humans start at this sight!' she smiled. 'You always think it is your death coming for you. But this isn't death, although your race once probably thought it was.'

'What is it then?' rasped Maddy.

'Not what, but who,' said Liadan. 'This is a member of the Coranied, a race of warlocks who ruled the Celts through fear. Now, ironically enough, they are slave masters for the Morrighan.'

'How?'

'Dark faeries, who are mostly my subjects, get their strength from chaos and disorder,' said Liadan. 'All the darkest, ugliest emotions and thoughts that humans and faeries can have – that's what my court feeds on. War in particular provides us with an opportunity to gorge ourselves. But the Coranied have a unique talent. They can gather up all those bad feelings, all those nightmarish places we go to in our heads, and they can store them, control them. Which means they can control us. They can keep us weak by rationing all those emotions, and the Morrighan can keep her pathetic peace.

'If I can cross into this world with my court, there's no Coranied to stop us,' she continued. 'We can feed on all the bad stuff going on in your world right now and don't even have to start a war. And I'll be strong as a Tuatha and able to bear the weight of this crown. And you are the key to all of this.'

'What are you talking about?' asked Maddy.

'You are a rare jewel, Maddy – a child who desires to die,' said Liadan. 'You are so full of rage and grief and hate. As pathetic as humans are, the will to live is the strongest urge, the last light to be snuffed out, and children cling to it hardest of all. Do you realize the power you create when you reverse that? The chaos? I've been trying to create that chaos with the children I've taken over the years, tried to torture them to the brink of death, but they all resisted. But with you I didn't have to do a thing.'

'You're lying,' said Maddy.

'No, I'm not,' said Liadan. 'Stephen was never the child we wanted, Maddy. It was always you. You're an agent of destruction, a walking curse, and we've been feeding off you ever since you set foot in our world. It is you who gave us the strength to get this far, to make it to the place between the worlds. Now you can help us step across.'

'How can I do that?' asked Maddy. 'I can't get across myself.'

'I just need you to hand your mind over to me and let me unleash that chaos. I'll do the rest.'

Maddy laughed. 'Why on earth would I do that?'

Liadan leaned closer. 'Because I can give you what you crave most . . . in any world. I can give you your parents back.'

Maddy stared at her, open-mouthed. The snow whirled gently down to coat their heads. 'No, you really are lying now,' she whispered hoarsely. 'You can't raise the dead.'

'Watch,' said Liadan.

Blackness covered Maddy's eyes. She cried out, her eyes straining in their sockets, and then she smelt her mother's perfume. She felt a hand settle on her shoulder and another smooth her hair back from her face and tuck it behind one ear, just like her mother used to do. Sounds and smells rushed toward her, and her head was flooded with a bright light.

She was standing in the kitchen of their house in London. Her father was cooking dinner and her mother was sitting at the table reading out loud from the newspaper. They were discussing the article, smiles hovering around their lips. Maddy stood and watched them, tears pouring down her face. Her mother glanced up and saw her and put the newspaper down on the table, her face full of concern. Her father broke off in mid-sentence and turned to face her, frowning. 'Maddy, darling, what's wrong?' he asked.

Maddy just cried harder, but a smile spread across her face at the same time. She was about to run forward and throw herself into his arms when the scene in front of her began to dissolve and recede, like water disappearing down a plughole. Just before her fingertips brushed the soft cotton of her father's T-shirt, she was left alone in the darkness again.

'NO!' she screamed. She bent double, her face pressed against the wet grass of the mound. 'Give them back, give them back . . .' Sobs wracked her body. The pain from her wound spread down and out and sapped her strength.

'I will, Maddy. Of course I will,' soothed Liadan. 'All you have to do is hand yourself over to me. Let your mind be my bridge into the mortal world and you can live your life here, between them. You will never be apart from your parents again. You'll never get any older and they will never die. Isn't that what you want?'

'What will happen to everyone here?' Maddy asked.

Liadan waved her hand, a look of contempt on her face. 'What do you care? Nothing will ever touch you again. You'll never have to hear another human voice, apart from your parents.'

Maddy looked down at the frozen ground and bit her lip until hot salty blood ran down her chin. She thought of Granny sewing by the fire, Mr and Mrs Forest and that house full of tumbling, loud, laughing boys and the smells of good things to eat. She thought of George and the way he smelt after they walked in the rain, his rough warm tongue on her face. She thought of Stephen's hot hand sliding into hers on a summer day, sticky with ice cream. She thought of Fionn's silvery fingers falling on snow. She thought of her parents again and fresh tears poured down her face. Granda was pressed against the faerie barrier, his eyes locked on to hers.

Whatever a faerie promises you, whatever they try to tempt you with, it's not real, said his voice in her head. *You have to trust your heart, not your eyes, and turn your feet for home.*

'Maddy, look at me,' said Liadan, her voice as soft as a snake's hiss. 'Look into my eyes and I can give you your life back.'

Maddy shifted off one knee and got her foot underneath her body. She looked at Liadan.

'Shove it,' she wheezed.

'What did you say?' said Liadan, her eyes narrowing in rage.

'I said shove it, Tinkerbell,' said Maddy. 'You're full of it, and if you think I'm letting you run around my head then your lift isn't reaching the top floor.' As soon as the words were out of her mouth Maddy lunged forward.

It almost worked. The barrier shivered as her

shoulder pierced it and for a brief moment she felt the wet drumming of rain on the back of her head, before a piercing cold enveloped her and she was yanked back on to the mound. Liadan leaned over her and gripped her ribs in her hands, ice rippling from her fingertips to coat Maddy's chest. Maddy screamed in agony and her body jerked like a fish on a line. Liadan sat up, panting with rage, while Maddy moaned, half unconscious with pain. The rest of the Winter Court was coming toward her now. She heard the whisper of a blade being drawn from a scabbard. Fachtna.

'You vicious, feral child,' snarled Liadan. 'I show you your heart's desire and you spit in my face? You have been offered more than any mortal ever has, and you insult me?!'

Soft white boots crunched through the snow to stop by Maddy's head. A silver blade hovered just by her ear. Liadan leaned down and placed her hand over Maddy's heart. Maddy almost blacked out. She listened to her own screams as if from a distance. Her heart withered in her chest, the ice sending shock after shock through it. Liadan pulled her hand away and Maddy retched.

'I will give you one more chance before I hand you over to Fachtna,' said Liadan. 'It's a very simple choice to make: give me what I want and I will give you your heart's desire; refuse me and you die.'

Maddy's hand went to her side and she felt something in her jacket pocket shift beneath her fingertips.

'I can have anything I want?' she asked, her voice small and trembling.

'Anything you want,' said Liadan, her face almost softening, but a glint of triumph flashing cold in her gaze.

Slowly Maddy unzipped her jacket pocket and slid her hand inside. 'Do you know what I really want?' she said.

'Tell me, child,' said Liadan, leaning closer, 'and I will make it so.'

Maddy turned her head so she could whisper into the faerie's curled ear.

'Shelves.'

Liadan stared at her, her eyes wide with disbelief, just as Maddy lifted her hand to her mouth and swallowed a fistful of iron filings. Flat on her back on the mound, Maddy could feel the vibrations of lingering magic. She concentrated on the hot rage that bubbled up from the pit of her stomach and flooded her throat, melting the iron filings, turning them to a liquid that flooded her veins, pushing back the cold and the pain.

'What have you done?' said Liadan, as she scrambled away from her. 'WHAT HAVE YOU DONE?'

Maddy lifted her hand and watched the iron turn her

veins grey. Her skin pulsed as the iron leached out of her pores, and even her eyes changed as a grey film covered her pupils and tainted everything she looked at.

She sat up and laughed, a hollow sound that rang like a bell in her chest. Then she dug her fingers through the snow and hooked them into the soil beneath her, which softened before the heat of her touch. The faerie mound heaved and cracked as it tried to spit out her taste. All around, the faeries were in chaos, trying to stay in control of panicking mounts, who reared as the iron poison licked at their feet from the polluted earth. The fir dorocha were beating a hasty retreat, the hounds fleeing ahead of them. Liadan was climbing on to her own mount, an animal cloaked in silver to protect it from her cold. The terrified animal tried to spin away and she yanked its head around viciously to face Maddy as the rest of her Winter Court stampeded for the opening in the mound. Blood foamed from its mouth and dripped on to its white chest. The only faerie who wasn't running in panic was Fachtna, who stood and stared at Maddy with a frown on her face. Maddy thought she saw a flicker of fear in the faerie's eyes. She grinned and got to her feet.

'Not so tough now, are you?' she said.

Liadan pointed a trembling finger at Maddy and screamed, 'Kill her, kill her now!'

Maddy laughed. She flexed her arms as the molten iron melted the last of the cold in her body and swallowed the pain. 'Come on then!' she yelled. 'Come and have a go, if you think you're hard enough!'

She barely had time to raise her arm to protect herself as Fachtna's sword came crashing down.

She grunted with surprise and staggered back, sparks flying as the blade scraped against her skin. Fachtna came at Maddy, swinging and stabbing and driving her back toward the mound opening. Maddy couldn't stand under the force of the faerie's blows and began to crumble to her knees. Fachtna raised her sword as if to strike down, and as Maddy lifted an arm to ward her off again, the faerie kicked her hard, throwing her on to her back. She planted a foot on Maddy's chest and raised her sword again.

The lightning from Maddy's world lit up Fachtna's face as she gripped the pommel with both hands. She bared her triangular teeth, her wings stiff and quivering behind her as her muscles bunched to drive the blade into Maddy's throat.

'You can't kill me!' screamed Maddy. 'Not with the iron in me!'

'Let's find out,' said Fachtna as she hurled the blade downwards. Maddy caught it in her hands and tried to hang on, the metal screaming and her skin sparking as Fachtna forced it through her palms. As Maddy's grey hands slid up toward the hilt, she lunged forward, letting the point of the sword bend against her skin, and grabbed Fachtna's wrist.

The effect was electrifying. The sword slid from Fachtna's frozen fingers and toppled from Maddy's one-handed grip. The faerie began to scream, a high-pitched noise like a rabbit in a trap. Where Maddy's iron fingers grasped her, the skin turned black and began to blister and bubble. Fachtna collapsed on to the earth and twisted and kicked in an attempt to shake Maddy off.

One booted foot caught Maddy a sharp blow in the ribs and she grunted and lost her grip on Fachtna's wrist. The faerie spun round to face her, panting. She went for one of the knives strapped across her chest, but when Maddy shouted, 'Stop!' Fachtna paused, her breath hissing through her filed teeth.

'It's over,' said Maddy. 'I made it home before you could catch me. Keep your word. Let me go.'

Fachtna narrowed her eyes at her. 'You're not home yet,' she snarled.

'Yes, I am,' said Maddy. She stretched out her hand, palm up. 'Look.'

The snow tumbled out of the air now, fatter and heavier. It was quickly turning to slush. As Fachtna lifted her sharp face to the sky, it began to pelt her with raindrops. The grey started to leak away from Maddy's skin.

'I think someone's been playing tricks on you,' said Maddy. 'Time has passed a lot quicker out here than in your world. The sun is coming up and the Samhain Fesh is over. This earth is in my world now. Keep your word.'

Fachtna glared at her. For a moment, Maddy thought the faerie would still try to slide a blade into her now soft throat as the magic faded and the iron retreated back to the filings in her stomach. But Fachtna turned away without a word, picked up her sword and followed her comrades into the mound, her injured hand curled against her chest. She walked into the darkness without a backwards glance. Liadan hovered by the entrance and hissed 'Coward' at her retreating back. She turned her dead white gaze on Maddy.

'I'll find you again, Maddy, mark my words,' she spat. 'You are a burden on those who love you, a walking curse. Hide under a mountain of iron and I will still find the hate and anger that boil around you and I will pull you loose, like a badger from its sett. And you know what we do with badgers, don't you?' She smiled her hideous smile, before yanking the reins and spurring her mount into the darkness of the mound.

Maddy stood up on the crushed and bloodied grass, not daring to believe it was over. Long fingers of sunlight trickled through the lower reaches of the trees as the sun rose. The air was filled with a rumbling noise as the mound began to close over. Granda ran past her with the howling changeling, which he flung into the dark just as the earth sealed itself. Weakness spread through Maddy and Granda rushed to catch her as she fainted. The last thing she remembered was vomiting up the iron filings.

chapter twenty-four

Maddy was standing in the village square a few days later, throwing a stick for George with Stephen, when a shadow fell across her. She smiled at the outline of antlers in the grass in front of her and turned around.

'Hiya, Seamus,' she said.

Seamus Hegarty smiled. 'How are you feeling, Maddy?'

'Not too bad, considering I've had your wife tenderizing me,' she said.

'And the wound in your shoulder?'

'It's scabbing over,' she said. 'It still hurts like mad, but you know, it could be worse.'

'That it could,' said Seamus.

They stood there in silence while Stephen squealed with delight, his chubby chocolate-covered hands snatching at the terrier's tail. George's tongue lolled against the stick as he ran rings around the toddler.

'How's the wee man?' asked Seamus, nodding at Stephen.

Maddy frowned. 'So-so,' she said. 'He doesn't seem to remember anything, but he has been having nightmares.'

Seamus grunted. 'He'll be OK,' he said. 'Children that small forget quickly. Has anyone been asking any questions?'

'No, but that has more to do with the fact that we got back on Halloween night,' she said. 'Handy that, seeing as it ties in with the whole theory that Stephen's been sleepwalking. I could have sworn we were in that mound for at least two days.'

'Very handy,' agreed Seamus, folding his arms across his chest and clamming up again. Maddy rolled her eyes.

'Come on, spit it out – how did you manage that?' she demanded.

'Time doesn't move in a straight line, the way you people think it does,' he said. 'It's a circle, and on the night of the Samhain Fesh it collapses into chaos. When there's chaos, you can change all the rules.'

'So I've heard,' said Maddy. She thought for a little while, working up the courage for her next question.

'So, any chance you're going to get a divorce any time soon?'

Seamus gave her a look from the corner of his eye. 'Things are bit more complicated than that.'

'That sounds hopeful,' she said. 'That's the kind of thing people say when they are getting a divorce. Along with, "Mummy and Daddy still really love you."'

'And how would you know?'

'I've got friends.'

'Have you indeed?'

Maddy blushed. 'Yeah, well, I have some now. Things have got a bit better lately.'

'So I've heard.'

She looked at him and grinned.

'You know what I've come to talk to you about, don't you, Maddy?'

Her smile faded and she nodded. 'Granda said you might be dropping by to have a word.' George came bounding up to her and dropped the stick at her feet. Stephen clutched at her jeans, leaving dirty smears on the denim, and peeped shyly at Seamus from around Maddy's thigh. Maddy bent and picked up the stick, and as she hefted it in her hand George twirled on his back legs with excitement.

'Stephen, do you think you can run faster than George?' asked Maddy, stroking his sweaty blond hair back from his forehead. Stephen nodded eagerly. 'If I throw this stick, do you think you can beat George to it?'

'A race?' asked Stephen, his face lighting up.

'Exactly, a race,' said Maddy. 'If you win, you get another square of chocolate.'

'Yay!'

'OK, ready . . . steady . . . GO!' Maddy swung her arm back and flung the stick as hard as she could. George tore after it, Stephen running awkwardly in his wake.

'How much chocolate has he had already?' asked Seamus.

Maddy turned to glare at him. 'Nowhere near enough to make up for everything that's happened to him.'

'Fair enough,' said Seamus, looking embarrassed.

Maddy watched Stephen's bright hair as he stumbled after George. She kept her gaze fixed on the little boy as she said, 'Tell me quick, before he comes back.'

'Your eyes are open now and you are Seeing,' said Seamus. 'That makes you a target. You've got to keep yourself safe and mind the rules. You know what goes on around here now, and solitary faeries are always about. There's no telling what they might do, when they are not part of a court and have no monarch to control them.'

'Is Stephen in any danger?' Maddy asked. 'Will they try to take him again?'

'Stephen's safe enough,' said Seamus. 'He was never the one Liadan wanted in the first place. They've been watching you, Maddy. They *knew* you would come after him. And I can't be looking after you every second of the day.'

She shrugged. 'I know.'

The autumn sun was warm on their faces, and the shouts of children playing circled them. George was crouched in front of Stephen, teasing the child with the stick. Every time Stephen made a grab for it, the dog whirled away, only to crouch down again, tail wagging.

As the quiet began to stretch between them, Seamus sighed. 'I can hear your brain working, Maddy. It's not very subtle. Why don't you just ask?'

'Everyone we met in there thought you were a big deal,' she said. 'They all went wobbly at the sound of your name. So why didn't you help us? Why didn't you get Stephen back yourself?'

'It's complicated . . .'

Maddy scowled. 'I nearly died, and you tell me it's *complicated* . . .'

'OK, fine, it's *politics*,' said Seamus. 'If I don't want someone interfering with the way I run things, I can't interfere with the courts. It's all about balance. If all the Tuatha leave each other alone, there will be no fighting. If I start trying to order around other Tuatha regents or the members of their court, it gives them an excuse to start an argument. But it doesn't mean I can't give things a nudge.'

'Like telling Granda what's going on?' she asked. 'Is that what you two are always talking about?'

'Yes.'

'And it was you that told him when we were coming back out and to meet us at the mound so he could swap that changeling?'

'Precisely,' said Seamus. 'You need to go easy on your granda, Maddy. He's been living in the shadow of the mound all his life. He knows only to be fearful. He lost your mother, and you're such a target . . . well, you can't blame the man for being cautious.'

'Liadan said I was an agent of destruction. Is that true?'

'There's something about you, Maddy, that sends ripples through our world. You're the key to something . . .'

'What?' prompted Maddy.

'That I don't know yet,' said Seamus. 'I think life will be more exciting with you around, but whether or not you're an agent for destruction, well, that's for you to decide.'

'Why *do* you hang around here so much?' asked Maddy.

Seamus looked down at her and grinned, full moons

floating in his eyes. 'I think it's an exciting world. Humans, you're changing all the time, and faerie kind never do. It's fun to watch.'

'Oh,' said Maddy. 'Well, I'm glad we make such good pets.'

Seamus frowned. 'That's not what I said.'

'I know, I know.' She held up her hands. 'I just don't believe your tourist story, but that's fine. I'm sure I'll get the truth another time.'

'The *truth* is that when I bound myself to the land, all those thousands of years ago, it was a mistake to let my strength wax and wane with the seasons,' said Seamus. 'It was a *huge* mistake to return to animal form in the winter. I thought it would keep me humble. All it did was make me weak at certain times of the year. Putting part of myself here, in the mortal world, is my insurance policy against trouble. I might only be a shadow of what I really am, but at least I can watch what goes on over there and in this world. As I said, it lets me give things a nudge.'

'Are things that bad between faeries and humans?' asked Maddy.

He sighed. 'Let's put it this way – powerful beings should never sleep. Not if they care.'

Maddy looked at her watch. 'I'd better get home,' she said.

'Busy afternoon?'

'Yeah, I'm helping Granda put up some shelves in my room.'

She whistled for George, and Stephen came panting up to her, his face crumpled and on the verge of tears.

'What's the matter, nappy bum?' she asked.

'Didn't win,' Stephen sobbed. 'No chocolate.'

'Oh, don't worry about that,' said Maddy as she reached down and lifted the child on to her hip, his arms circling her neck. 'You came second and second prize is also a bar of chocolate.'

She nodded a goodbye to Seamus and walked across the square, George trotting by her side, his teeth firmly clamped around the stick. As she got to the wall that divided the village square from the street, she turned to look. Seamus was still standing where she had left him, his face up to the sunlight, a full spread of antlers only she and a handful of others could see dipping down his back.

Stephen yanked a handful of hair. 'Maddeeee,' he whinged. 'Wan' go home.'

She hugged him tight. 'So do I,' she whispered into his hair.

gLossary

Aoife (ee-fa) – A GLAISTIG, and lady-in-waiting to Queen LIADAN.

Cernunnos (ker-noo-nos) – One of the oldest and most powerful of the TUATHA DE DANNAN, he clings to the form he took when he was worshipped in pre-Christian Ireland, the horned god. But he likes to linger in our world too, so he takes on human form for the winter months, calls himself Seamus (shay-mus) and lives in Blarney, Co. Cork, keeping an eye on the mortal world and any comings and goings from TÍR NA NÓG. It's a weird way to spend your holidays, but who's going to argue with an ancient Celtic god?

Dullahan (doo-la-han) – A very nasty dark faerie, the headless dullahan is a soul collector. Sometimes he rides a giant black horse, other times a coach and six horses. He never speaks, except to say the name of the person whose soul he has come to collect. No door or gate can be barred against him.

Fachtna (fakht-na) – Means 'hostile' in Irish. Says it all really. Fachtna lives, eat, sleeps and breathes war. Never happier then when she has a knife in her hand.

Fionn (Fee-on) – A dryad, which is an elemental faerie, the soul of her tree. Elementals are simple creatures, and the other faeries tend to look down on them for it.

Fionnula (fin-oo-la) – Not a faerie, but Maddy's very human aunt. You would not want to bump into her in a dark alleyway though.

Fir Dorocha (fear dor-ka) – Means 'dark men' in Irish. These faeries are the embodiment of fear. They spread hatred and terror before them and drive mortals crazy. Wherever there is a mob or a riot in progress, the fir dorocha are close by. They have also been known to abduct mortals for the kings and queens they serve. Basically, they do all the nasty jobs LIADAN and the TUATHA do not want to do themselves. Faeries to avoid at all costs.

Gancanagh (Gan-cah-nah) – Maddy is lucky that no matter how gorgeous she thinks Connor is, she's too young to be interested in kissing boys (yuck!). Connor is a gancanagh, a male faerie who has a poison in his skin that makes mortal women fall in love with him forever. When he leaves them, they die pining for him. One kiss is enough.

Glaistig (glay-steeg) – Glaistigs are either hostile or friendly, depending on who you are. Normally they lurk near water and lure male travellers to their deaths. They are not very keen on men. But they love children, so much so that mortal women often used to let a local glaistig care for their children while they washed their clothes in the river. Stephen is very lucky to have been cared for and surrounded by glaistigs in Queen LIADAN's court. Any faerie that might have tried to harm him would have found the fingers of AOIFA or her sisters wrapped around their throat.

Liadan (lee-ah-dan) – Means 'grey lady' in Irish. Liadan is an old and powerful elf from the Nordic countries. No one knows why she and her clan came to TÍR NA NÓG seeking sanctuary, but she's as argumentative as the TUATHA DE DANNAN. Do you know someone in school who could start a fight in an empty room? That's Liadan. The only good thing about her is that she unites the TUATHA against her. Everyone needs someone to hate, right?

Morrighan (more-i-gan) – In pre-Christian Ireland the Morrighan was worshipped as a triple-faced goddess. She represents the maiden, the mother and the crone and is the most powerful of the TUATHA DE DANNAN. It is her power that created TÍR NA NÓG and her power alone that keeps the boundaries up between the faerie and mortal worlds. The Morrighan is also one of the most dangerous of the TUATHA. She is also known as the Raven Queen and is the living embodiment of war. Waking the Morrighan is not something that should be done lightly.

Roisin (roe-sheen) – Maddy's cousin. If she doesn't know the answer, she'll google it. Might get a bit panicky but generally a good person to have in your corner.

Samhain Fesh (sow-en fesh) – This was the pagan feast that marked the start of winter, when the harvest was gathered in and people got ready to endure the winter months. It is also the time of year when the boundaries between the faerie world, TÍR NA NÓG, and the mortal world wear thin and faeries can cross over to us and we can find ourselves lost in their realm. Christians tried to stamp out Samhain by replacing it with All Hallows Eve or Halloween, but the old ways are there, underneath it all, even if we have forgotten them. So the next time you go trick-or-treating, put a cross around your neck and some iron in your pocket. And always be nice to old ladies you meet on the road – you never know who you are talking to. Faeries never forget a kind deed or a harshly spoken word.

Sean Rua (shawn roo-a) – This is a faerie as old as the TUATHA DE DANNAN. He has been mentioned in folklore for thousands of years and seems to pledge allegiance to any court he feels like serving at the time. No one knows exactly what Sean Rua is, but his talent is that he resembles a child and has hypnotic powers of persuasion. He has lured hundreds, if not thousands, of mortals beneath the mounds, and there is no record of any of them returning home.

Selkies – You have heard of werewolves? Well, there are actually lots of werepeople and other animals in the world. Selkies are seals. They can shed their seal fur on land and change into a person. If you take a seal-woman's fur she has to follow you home, and as long as you keep her sealskin away from her she has to stay a woman and cannot go home to the sea. Quite a nasty thing to do to a selkie, no? So don't do it. Ever.

Tír na nÓg (teer na nogue) – The Land of Eternal Youth. The fabled realm of the TUATHA DE DANNAN that exists beneath Ireland's surface, the place they fled to when they lost their battles against mortals for control of Ireland. This is where the TUATHA and the lesser tribes of faeries live. Many, many people search for ways in, but you need a faerie guide to enter the realm and getting out is never as easy. Something to think about if you have things urgent to do topside – I'd clear your diary.

Tuatha de Dannan (too-ay day dah-nan) – The Tuatha have many names: the Shining Ones, the Fair Folk, the Gentry. Some call them faeries, but they call themselves gods. They used to be in charge of Ireland, until St Patrick came along, and they have serious powers. They can control all the elements – air, water, fire and earth – cast powerful spells and change their form at will. They are vain and short-tempered, cruel and spiteful. They argue so much that fighting has practically become a hobby. They are the most powerful beings in TÍR NA NÓG and they rule it. It's best not to upset them.